Dear V,

Hope you enjoy reading the book oh, make Lee read it to!

Dont stop being Cool

Luvs ya

Estaban +xx
10/8/07

Trilogy of Leon

Hope, Faith and Love

Estaban Bridges

Bloomington, IN authorHOUSE® Milton Keynes, UK

AuthorHouse™
1663 Liberty Drive, Suite 200
Bloomington, IN 47403
www.authorhouse.com
Phone: 1-800-839-8640

AuthorHouse™ UK Ltd.
500 Avebury Boulevard
Central Milton Keynes, MK9 2BE
www.authorhouse.co.uk
Phone: 08001974150

© 2007 Estaban Bridges. All rights reserved.

No part of this book may be reproduced, stored in a retrieval system, or transmitted by any means without the written permission of the author.

First published by AuthorHouse 4/24/2007

ISBN: 978-1-4259-9418-1 (sc)

Printed in the United States of America
Bloomington, Indiana

This book is printed on acid-free paper.

I dedicate this novel to all those with hope in each other,
Faith in there own lives and love for life itself.

Dedicated to Christa.

My thanks to my brothers and sisters for being the best.

My thanks to my parents for keeping me on track over the years.

All my love to Vicky.

Finally my greatest of respect to;
Kyle Bailey and Rob Lisney
for helping me get where I am.

Contents

Part I: Born a Hero. A heavenly soul.

Darkness arrives
1

The Rescue
7

The journey home
13

Meeting the mother
23

Winning back home
29

Leon, the people's person
37

Defending freedom
45

The return of Thain
53

Hopes death
59

Revenge for a loved one.
67

The eye of the storm.
73

Part 2: Hero Reborn A Soul Worth Returning..

Hero Reborn A soul worth returning

Part I

Born a Hero.

A Heavenly Soul.

Darkness arrives

How many warriors does it take to end a war? The answer is simply too many. One hero, one legend, one man can end all suffering and slaughter. This hero has been born.

Darkness covers the vast land. Black clouds rule the sky. Battles of magic are fought between wizards and sorceresses. Battles of land are fought between armies. The battle for love and happiness has been all but lost apart from in one small village in the middle of a large flat stretch of land. It is here in which a hero was born.

A sunny late afternoon and all is calm in a small village called Savon. Wind blows ever so gently; rustling leafs of the tall trees. Children play happily in the corn fields. The men of the village build new huts. They plough the fields and merrily go about daily tasks. The women prepare a great dinner to be held in the village hall to celebrate a successful season for the crops. Everybody is happy and there is a large unbreakable amount of love between them all.

Estaban Bridges

It begins to darken across the land with rain clouds covering the sun. Rain starts to drip but still everything stays calm and peaceful. The people of the village escape the rain and collect together in the village hall.

A young beautiful mother hugs her child as the village chief; Saridus kisses her softly upon her cheek. The beautiful woman pushes Saridus the silent smiling child. The child was reluctant to go to him but walked over to him anyway. Saridus addresses all of the villagers now sitting at large tables. With a strong voice he gives a speech,

"My fellow villagers listen closely now to the words I speak. The land in which we live, the land in which we share, is soon and guaranteed to be taken away from us and for this my friends I apologize. I was once a strong man who was full of courage and could defend against temptation. Now I am nothing more than a broken leader but yet you all stay so strong. You all stay together so close and with such passion. For this I applaud you." Saridus claps his hands slowly and quietly as he smiles at his people and he lifts his wine. The villagers laugh and cheer with each other although the majority of them did not really understand what he was saying,

"May today, my friends, be remembered and loved by us all." With the end of Saridus saying this, the cheering becomes louder and the feast begins.

Time flows by quickly as it reaches the mid hour. The rain now falls hard upon the village. The wind blows violently and constantly. Thunder roars after the sharp lightning. A loud knock beckons the large doors of the hall. All goes silent. The villagers stare at the doors, all of them waiting in extreme suspense.

The large wooden doors become ajar. They open fully revealing a shadowed figure. Still all is silent apart from the patter of the rain upon the roof and the thunder drifting from the distance. The strange shadowed figure takes a step forward through the doors into the light of the hall. Standing before them was a large built man. He had long straight dark hair. Light green blood shot eyes and his face was as dirty as the wet ground. He wore a long black cape which was heavily torn and shredded. His chest covered in a battered beyond recognition metal vest. His trousers were black and also torn slightly with a symbol of a dragon along the left leg, the symbol of a black magic wizard. In his hand he held an old staff. Engraved onto it was a snake. From the bottom, was its tail and it went to its head at the top. The snakes head had its mouth wide open and from it a large flame smoked continuously. The mysterious man spoke with a deep voice,

"Well what a night villagers." The man smiles, "What a good night to die." Shocked the villagers gasp and begin to shuffle slightly. Panic was quickly beginning to start amongst them all. Saridus stands from the thrown he was sat,

"What is the meaning of this intrusion? Who are you?" The man looks up at Saridus,

"Saridus, my, my, my, you don't cease to amaze me." The caped stranger lifts his snake engraved staff as a signal. Suddenly from behind him soldier after soldier emerge. They wore similar cloths as the caped man. The soldiers ran against the walls of the hall and they totally surround the villagers. They withdrew there swords and stood straight with the swords by there sides.

By now the villagers begin to panic wildly. Like a chain reaction they all rise to there feet. Children start to cry. Females start to scream and hold the children close. The males move to protect both the children and the females. With a large smile of a crazy man the caped intruder shouts out,

"Ha, panic, pure panic I love it. You will never get away, never." The man leans his staff forward. As if under control the soldiers begin to close in on the villagers. Slaughtering them as they harvest there way through, killing them one by one. The villagers have no defense. No chance of survival. Screaming and howling, the sound of death and horror, murder and sorrow fills the air.

As this meaningless murder of so many innocent people takes place in front of the young mother's eyes she flees with her child behind where the thrones stood. Behind the thrones was a secret extremely well hidden passage leading to the rear of the hall connected to her and Saridus' own hut.

She runs as if she was drifting on air. Not looking back, scared of looking back. The screams of murder echo throughout the passage and finally she arrives at the exit. She opened an old doorway leading the way into the large hut that her and Saridus lived in and continued to flee toward the main entrance. She was confronted by a horrible burning image of the village as she left the front entrance. Every way in which she looked she saw bright tall fires desecrating the huts which made the village. The farm animals ran free stampeding to find safety. She falls devastated to her knees holding tight the child she was trying so desperately to protect.

Trilogy of Leon

A middle aged woman, dressed in a dirty apron and an old dress appears. She walks toward the doorway the mother was knelt in front of,

"My Lady," She spoke softly, her voice full of love and care,

"My Lady, what is happening? Why does the devil set fire upon our village like this?" The young mother stands looking into the eyes of the woman who stood before her,

"Please, take my child." The mother begs as tears of sadness and horror emerge from her eyes,

"Please, I beg you, take my child and run far away for they are coming and will find us soon." The mother holds the child out in invitation. In confusion the woman asks,

"But my lady, I do not understand, who is this that you speak of? Who has done this?" The mother becomes erratic,

"Please, please just take my child for soon it shall be to late, darkness has done this, darkness has found us. Run, now." The mother forces the child upon the woman and for a few short terrifying moments they stand in a motionless time. The mother takes a jewel from within her necklace and places it within the child's hand. With this the woman starts to run with the child in her tight possession. As they run the child looks back to take a final look at his mother as she is taken away by a wall of flames covering the path. The two companions escape undetected from the hell that used to be there home. A lone horse standing strong beyond the village gates becomes the life saving getaway. The horse was that of Saridus'. The horse was born when an old Wiseman's soul was sacrificed to be at Saridus' service. This was because Saridus had saved his life from the darkness but the old man died naturally, it was the old mans own option to give his soul to help Saridus as repayment for his help, until Saridus deemed it necessary to release him and let his soul free to go to the afterlife. The horse was immortal and was very strong. The woman and child gallop at the fastest of speeds through the fields and land beyond to find a new place, a place in which they can call home.

THE RESCUE

Ten years upon the burning of his home village the child now a man known as Leon lives as a farmer and a loving son to his new mother who took care of him as if he were her own since the day he had been thrown upon her. Leon cleans the stables of the savior horse as his mother collects drinking water from the nearby forest.

Life is calm. Cold clear water runs down a stretched stream. The green leafs shuffled gently in the easy breeze. Songs of the forest birds come from all around but then sudden silence.

The water which was once so cool and clear turns red as blood flows with the current. Standing tall, a man in the shadows of the trees. He turns without a care in the world and slowly starts to walk away from a woman's body lying in the stream, which was staining the water red with warm blood from a slash to the neck. As he disappears into the darkness of the silent forest his laughter echoes throughout.

Leon walks out of the stables to find a man standing looking away from him into the fields. The man wore a long black cape and had long dark hair with a sword upon his back. As Leon stands looking at the man he turns around. His face showed a long time of cuts and grazes. Large scars ran across his face all over. The man smiles,

"The son, how are you these glorious days?" Leon fairly confused replies,

"Who, who are you?" The man smile drops and he starts to walk toward Leon,

"I've always wanted to find you. All because your stupid witch of a mother gave you the one and only thing I wanted, that very shiny, little jewel in the chain around your neck. That's mine you know." Leon begins to step backward looking worryingly from left to right,

"If you're looking for that dreadful old woman, the one you must have grown to love. The one you grew to cherish, she's dead. Her bodies probably being shredded by a pack of wolfs as we speak." Leon's heart sinks at the thought of the loss of his family death, his mother's death. His body becomes heated and he becomes highly agitated,

"You lie; I refuse to believe the words you speak. Get away from me and leave my home." Leon shouts with rage and anger while the mystery man simply laughs,

"I pity you. You're not strong at all. You're weak with a minor touch of attitude. All these years I have thought more of you. Now that we have actually met, I am very much disappointed. I guess killing you isn't going to be as much a pleasure as I wish it would be. Ah well, I shall do it anyway." The man slowly draws his sword and starts a fast pace toward Leon. From as if out of nowhere a figure

Trilogy of Leon

appears on a large white horse from through the fields. As the figure approached it could be seen that it was another man wielding a large bow and arrow. Like a strike of lightning an arrow is released and it strikes the other stranger, pacing toward Leon, in the shoulder. Wounded the man turns from Leon growling in agony. As he turns he lifts his hand producing an endless blast of fire toward the horseman but magnificently before it had chance to crash into him he also raises his hand sending a protective wave of raging water which shields him from the offensive fire attack. The attack is withdrawn as it has no affect and the horseman speaks loudly,

"It's not like you to travel somewhere alone Thain. Leave the young man alone or I will, don't think I'm bluffing but I will rip you apart." The man, now recognized as Thain snaps the arrow in his shoulder and turns once again to face Leon. He starts to run at Leon and lifts his sword to strike him while letting out an almighty roar. As he is about to strike his forceful blow he is swept from the ground as if he were nothing more than a leaf and thrown across the floor at great speed. With a great thump he lands. He kneels trying to come back to his senses and looks up at the horseman, in a crackling voice he snarls,

"You've got stronger since our last encounter Lord Shione but ever more careless." As Thain finishes his sentence he stands and raises his hand in a blink of an eye, suddenly a large wall of mud and stone spikes up through the ground splitting any connection between Lord Shione and Leon. With the divide in place Thain points his other hand directly at Leon and as soon as he does so a vine of pure lightning wraps around him making his body collapse and fall to the floor. His body shakes violently with shock as the lightning traps him. Thain shouts smiling apparently victorious,

"But Shione I am always so powerful." While keeping up the two excessive moves of extreme magic a small gust of wing starts to blow. The wall of mud and stone breaks apart by a whirlwind produced around Lord Shione. The rubble of the wall was rotating at breathtaking speed. With an enormous thunder the whirlwind catapults the remains of the wall toward Thain. It collides straight into him knocking him at an instant to the ground therefore the shocking connection he had upon Leon. Completely dazed by the assault Thain tries to regain his balance and so Lord Shione takes the perfect opportunity to gallop toward Leon who remained shaking on the ground. As Lord Shione reaches Leon he lifts him from the ground and places him upon his horse. They ride to the forest in which his foster mother had been killed, leaving Thain behind them, recovering to rise again from the magical exchange.

Lord Shione upon the horse with Leon reaches the stream where the body of the murdered woman lay. Lord Shione steps to the damp ground and pulled Leon to his feet. By now the effect of the shock of lightning had nearly wore off and Leon was getting his senses back. Lord Shione checks his eyes,

"You recover fast. You are strong after all." Leon looks down to see the body in the stream and like a flash runs to her side,

"Mother, mother," He sobbed as he clutched her close. Leon looks up at Lord Shione standing by his side,

Trilogy of Leon

"You, you knew that man, he knew your name, Lord Shione. What is the reason this has happened?" Lord Shione places his hand upon leon's shoulder,

"Please, you may call me Shione. There is much for you to learn. We have far to go. I have someone special for you to see so come with me for now you must become who you're meant to be." Leon turns his head,

"You talk no sense. I will not go. I shall stay to care for the farm." Shione looks down as he shakes his head,

"Your farm is most certainly being burnt down right now. There is nothing keeping you here anymore." Leon looks horrified at Shione,

"Not the farm, not my home. Savior, not him to?" A tear rolls down his cheek, a tear full of every bad emotion. Shione smiles,

"Don't give into sadness before you see the truth for maybe your horse will be alive. I saw a horse run from your stables as Thain attacked us." Shione puts out his hand,

"Place out your hand and repeat your horses name. I will be able to tell you if he is alive and well plus I can bring him back to you." With mild believe in Shione's words Leon puts out his hand still holding the still body of the woman. Leon begins to repeat,

"Savior, Savior." Shione places his hand on top of Leon's and closes his eyes. He tilts his head up toward the sky and after a short pause looks back down at Leon,

"Savior is on his way to you." Leon smiles slightly with relieve and looks down at the body he held. Shione gently mentions while stepping backward toward his horse,

"Maybe you should let her be now." Leon places the body onto the ground and looks back at Shione,

"I must rest her soul to sleep Shione. It's the least I could do." Shione turns and walks a little further to his horse,

"I am sorry but if I let you take the time to do that then we shall both die. Thain will be coming after us and this time he won't be alone. We must go, now." Leon slowly stands as from behind him amazingly his large well groomed moon white horse, Savior appears from within the forest. The horse walks calmly over to Leon brushing itself on Leon's chest. Shione starts to ride away and shouts behind him back at Leon,

"Will you follow your destiny or drown in your sorrow. Stay and be killed or ride and be alive. You can only make that choice. You must decide." Leon takes a short moment to think and climbs upon Savior. He takes one more glance at the innocent dead body lying next to the stream in the soft mud. He turns his head. A new start. Leon begins to race so that he could catch up with Shione before he disappeared through the forest.

3

THE JOURNEY HOME

They both travel side by side over the vast lands which they need to cover. Without sleep and with the rare rest they travel through forests and across plain fields. With great haste they travel over streams and through rivers. Riding night and day they never look back. Through the sun, the cold and the rain they glide like the wind. To where is a mystery to Leon but all soon to be explained. For where they arrive will be the place where the past will be revealed. For where they arrive a battle will arise. For where they arrive is the City of Savon, formally known as his home, the village of Savon. Around midday on a cold but dry day Leon and Shione exit a large forest from which they had been riding through and arrive on the side of a mountain. It was a fair distance away from a very large well built city.

The city was surrounded by a dirty moat with just one access point over which was a drawbridge. Beyond the drawbridge was a small stretch of land all around the city, leaving an area of empty land between the city and the moat.

The city had beautifully built walls towering high above the ground. From where the two companions were they could see a professional, well cared for and highly populated settlement. One building stuck out more than any other, a large palace directly in the middle of the city. Leon looks away from the city and turns to Shione,

"Shione, there is something hovering on my mind." Shione also turns and looks at Leon,

"What is that then?" Leon continues to explain,

"Well I have been thinking and we have rid all this way and yet we have not even spoken on our travels. I know your name but still you do not know mine. Also I have questions. For example why have you brought me to this place?" Shione steps down from his horse and kneels down on the ground looking back at the city,

"What is your name then?" Leon also steps down from savior and stands aside Shione,

"Leon, my name is Leon." Shione looks up at Leon beside him,

"Leon. Really, Lady Christa always wondered what your name was. I was sent by Lady Christa to find you. Luckily I found you just at the right time." Leon puzzled by the short explanation replies,

"But I do not know a Lady Christa and I have never seen this city before in my whole life. Why were you sent to find me like you have?" Shione stands without response and walks back toward the forest they had just left. He began to pick up dry sticks and came across a large log which he lifted and balanced on his shoulder. He turns

Trilogy of Leon

silently looking back at Leon standing there as he was before,

"Don't just stand there Leon. Help me find some good fire wood and I shall give you the answers you need to know. Before night fall we shall enter the city." Leon proceeds to help Shione with the collection of suitable wood while still confused about his new experience and trying to figure the situation out in his head.

A small fire burns and crackles as night beckons arrival on the land. The two men sit either side of the fire. Leon holds his hands closed near the fire trying to gain warmth as Shione adds small sticks to act as fuel. Shione sits back and rubs his hand across his chin in thought. He sits forward again,

"Listen carefully Leon because what I am about to tell you will make no sense at all to you in anyway, shape or form. You probably won't believe one word of the truth but I shall still go ahead and tell you. Understand?" Leon nods and puts his hand out showing for Shione to continue,

"The city you see down there is the City of Savon. Before this city, was built the village of Savon. It was here in which you were born. A planned attack was set upon the village and the village was set alight. The villagers were killed viciously by soldiers and your mother managed to flee too safely for a short time. She could not risk keeping you with her because she feared for your life. She gave you to the woman who you then grew up to believe was your mother. Once the village was turned to dust an army set foot here and the city of Savon was built in the matter of a few years as the capital of Savon, this being the perfect place to have a city. In the heart of the country the city is

Estaban Bridges

untouchable by far away enemies." Leon shakes his head smirking in disagreement,

"That is surely not true at all Shione. How come I have never known even the slightest detail of this? Who were the soldiers? If this is true then where is my mother? Answer these questions if you can?" Shione continues,

"Be open minded Leon, please. The attack was planned between the Darkness and some selected people in the village. The man who led this attack was Thain. Back then he was just a commander but now he is a general for the Darkness. You do not know of the past because you were too young to remember. I believe you were ten years old at the time it happened. The woman who took care of you did not tell you because she wanted to protect you from the truth." Leon looks down in disbelief but with some sort of understanding,

"My real mother and farther were killed in the attack?" Leon asks as he looks back up,

"Actually no Leon, they are both very much alive. I can take you to see your mother right now." As Shione said this he pointed toward the city,

"She isn't that far away from you. I see you still have the jewel around your neck. That is very pleasing. Your mother gave you that before you separated in the night of the attack. Apparently it is of great power." Leon holds the jewel in his hand,

"And this is why that man, Thain was after it. I think I'm beginning to understand and it's all making sense although I am still not fully convinced of your story. Shione, who is my mother? What is her name?" Shione smiles,

Trilogy of Leon

"Your mothers name is Lady Christa of Savon City. She is waiting for us in the palace you see. For this is her city now, Leon." Leon casts his eyes at the palace,

"But the village was originally taken by Darkness forces. So is my mother now one of them? If not then why is she the Lady of the capital city?"

"No your mother is not with the Darkness but she simply pretends to be. Your father is still alive, his name is Saridus. He is the one possessed by the darkness" Shione stands,

"The attack upon the village was planned between Thain, Saridus and a few of your fathers close companions. Thain promised a large city to be built and great fortune to be given. Thain kept to his word. Saridus had given into temptation and for this his own people suffered and now he has a larger role in the Darkness, therefore leaving your mother in charge of the city." Shione walks over to his horse,

"Leaving your mother in charge is no big deal to the darkness because there empire covers many lands and this is a small city compared to others. The secret is that this city is just supposed to be the capital but this city is a decoy for the real capital." Shione mounts his horse and grabs hold of the reins,

"Come Leon, meet your mother." Shione slowly starts to trot down the easiest way off the mountain. Leon climbs upon Savior and follows Shione thinking carefully about every detail he had been told.

They reach the bottom of the mountain and continue along the rough ground to the drawbridge which was currently being held up in the air so that the passage across was not open. Shione lifts his hood and placed it over his head. He also got a scarf and wrapped it around the bottom of his face so that only his eyes were visible. He whispers quietly to Leon,

"I cannot be seen here at the gate by the guards. The guards are those loyal to the Darkness. If Thain finds that I am here it will bring unrest and your mother will be questioned. We need to remain unnoticed for who we really are until we reach inside the palace. Things will change from then. Thain will be looking for us both and now that he knows I am with you he will more than likely be coming back here with his men to hunt us and here at the moment he is free to come and go as he pleases. I advice you hide your face to Leon." Following the advice from Shione Leon covers his face with his hood and looks down to try and hide slightly under the dimming light. As the drawbridge began to lower Leon questions Shione,

"Shione, how come you have battled with Thain before?" Shione quietly replies,

"In the palace your farther was away and so Thain took the opportunity to question your mother about the jewel. He attacked her to try and get her to release any information she may have had and so I intervened, I attacked him to protect your mother. I am technically Lady Christa's body guard and protector. That's how he will know Lady Christa had something to do with my appearance back at your farm." They became silent as the drawbridge lowered far enough so that Leon and Shione could see over to the other side of the moat. In there view they could see a group of ten soldiers. The bridge lowered fully and the ten soldiers began to walk over. They wore red and black untouched in battle armor. As they walked across they moved into two separate lined formations and stood either side of the bridge with there backs against the sides of the bridge. They withdrew there swords and held them by there sides. Another soldier emerged from where they had just come and walked between the two lines of soldiers. This man wore a large helmet and a large black cape. He was the squadron commander. The commander stood a short distance away from Shione and Leon looking at them both eyeing them all other for weapons,

"What brings you to the City of Savon strangers?" Shione replies hiding his voice in a deeper more crackling tone,

"I bring this slave to trade in the city for wheat and bread so I am able to feed my pregnant wife back at home officer." The man does not move and continues to stand staring at the two of them,

"I'm a commander. Not an officer, stupid old man. Also since when has a slave had the rights of being given a horse to ride, especially such a well built horse?" Shione crackles a quiet laugh,

"Officer, we have traveled an awfully long way. If I had made this skinny set of old bones walk I wouldn't have had a slave to trade at all." The commander stepped aside and waved his hand to his soldiers who raised there swords to there chests. The commander looks at Leon and Shione,

"You may proceed. Watch yourself old man. Times are dangerous for men like you to be traveling." Shione trots casually onto the drawbridge and Leon followers his lead. As they get further over the bridge the commander follows them and the line of soldiers walk behind them. They reach the other side, Leon and Shione continue toward the gates as the soldiers remain at the drawbridge.

The drawbridge was raised once again sealing them within the city perimeter with no way back.

The two of them travel towards the gates of the city without saying a word to each other. Slowly they ride over the empty marsh land between the drawbridge and city gates, looking to see of any sign of the gates opening. As to plan when they got nearer to the gates they opened with the creaking sound of old rusted hinges. The two of them enter the city and the gates are closed behind them. Large wooden logs used to barricade the door closed. Shione points ahead,

"Leon. There is the destination." Shione turns and looks through the crowded path following the direction he was pointing. The way led to a large set of steps which led the way to the large red doors of the city palace. Shione continues to instruct Leon,

"Don't look and stare at anybody in the street down here. They are all traders and we haven't got the time to stop and get into conversation so for now, keep yourself to yourself. Keep your head down and follow me." Shione trots ahead of Leon pushing his way through the many people rushing about and Leon followed closely. As they pass through the streets the city folk stare at them, eyeing them over for treasures or anything worth trading. Some of the merchants ran there hands over the body's of the horses they were riding to see if they were well fed and worth bargaining for. Eventually they reached the bottom of the palace steps leading up to the large doors. Shione dismounts and hands the reigns of his horse to a man standing guard who was wearing a different uniform than those of the soldiers at the drawbridge.

Trilogy of Leon

"From here Leon we shall not have any problems. The soldiers in the palace grounds, mostly around the city and within the palace are those of Lady Christa. They are loyal to the Lady and ready for the uprising. The city people are also all on our side. The lady has worked very hard to win everybody onto our side." Leon also dismounts from savior and hands the reins to the same guard Shione had handed his to, Leon places his hand upon the guards shoulder,

"Take good care of this guy he's very tired and hungry." The guard nods understanding the needs requested. Leon follows Shione walking slowly up the stairs. He looks around at the view as they got higher and higher up the stairs and then he takes a good look at the palace doors,

"Shione, how come the only men in black and red armour are the men at the drawbridge and the few which I can see are falling over themselves drunk beyond any normality?" They stop walking up the steps and they both look widely over the passageway they had just come through and any other visible area which they could see. Shione smiles at Leon,

"That is a very good point my friend. They have left themselves unguarded and got used to an easy atmosphere. Quick, we have to move. Now is the right time" Shione turns and starts to jog at a fast pace further toward the top of the steps as Leon stands confused, putting out his arms to show he was open for an explanation. He questions,

"Shione, the right time to do what exactly? What on earth are you talking about and why have the palace doors been stained red?" Shione runs back down a few steps and places his hand on Leon's shoulder,

"This is a great time, the perfect time. The perfect opportunity to over power the darkness forces which plague our city. We can force the very few dark soldiers out of the city therefore giving us the city which we so badly want to fight for. It will be in our full control. This is exactly what Lady Christa and the people of this city want. You want to know about the doors, the red which stained the doors was the blood of all the original villagers that were murdered. A reminder for the people to show what happened if you do not follow the darkness way of life. Quick, follow me" Shione pulls on Leon's shoulder and they both jog hastily to the top of the steps.

MEETING THE MOTHER

They reached the top of the steps and were greeted by four smart looking guards. They wore different armor than the guards at the drawbridge and generally better disciplined. One of the four guards steps forward and greets Shione by firmly shaking his hand,

"Greetings Lord Shione, were happy that you have returned safely. Its great to have you back." Shione smiles happily,

"Its great to be back my friend. Can you tell me; is the Lady Christa in her chamber?"

"Why yes she is my Lord. She has been waiting some what impatiently for your return." The guard invites Shione and Leon through the large palace doors which the other guards had previously opened in advance. As they calmly walk through the doors Shione pulls the soldier close. In a serious manner he talked to the guard,

"My friend, call upon the best of the royal guard. Get them quickly equipped and ready. Wait in the palace hall where we will meet you shortly. The time we've been waiting for has finally been presented to us." The man bowed his head and acknowledged the command. The guard turns and runs out toward the steps. As he travels down the steps the three other guards close the doors leaving Leon and Shione at the front entrance inside the palace. Shione pulls Leon along by his arm,

"Welcome home Leon." They continued to walk through the corridors and reached there destination. They stood in front of a set of two large wooden doors. They were engraved with gold patterns of dragons. Shione pointing at the doors said,

"Leon, inside this room is your mother. Are you ready for this?" Leon takes a long deep breath,

"Yes Shione I am." Shione knocks on the doors and pushes them open. Once open the two of them walk into a large room. Inside the room was a large bed against the one wall draped in soft silk cloth. A large cabinet sat against another wall and a single seat next to the door. Other than that the door was empty. Sitting at the cabinet looking into a mirror made into it was Leon's mother, Lady Christa. She was sitting with her back to the door combing through her long hazel brown hair. Shione knelt where he stood,

"My Lady, I have returned as you wished accompanied with your son, known as Leon." Lady Christa turned in her seat. She looked straight into Leon's eyes. With a great smile of pure happiness a tear rolled down the side of her smooth firm face. Leon remained standing where he had entered. He didn't say a word or make a move; he just stood looking amazed into Christa's eyes. Shione relieves himself from where he knelt. Turned he leaves the room

Trilogy of Leon

closing the door behind him. Lady Christa stood from her seat and slowly approached Leon. She ran her hand across the side of his face. Her soft gentle touch soothed him and made him slightly smile. She held Leon's hands with hers,

"You're as beautiful a man as I had always imagined." Leon put his arms around his mother and held her tight. A tear also ran down his cheek from his eye, tears of relief and happiness.

"Now I believe everything Shione has told me for I feel in my heart and my soul that what he said is true. Something pulls inside of me, pulls toward you. A feeling I have never felt before or never remembered. You are my mother and I am glad to have met you again." Lady Christa moves and holds his hands once again,

"I am so happy you have been taken care of Leon. I hope you do understand why I had to let you go that day? I had to let you go to save your life because it was more than likely going to be taken away from you and this I could not bare to think of." Leon nods his head still looking into her eyes,

"Yes mother I understand and I do not hold this against you. I am happy you have found me for now my heart feels as if it beats once again. A hole in my heart has been filled. I am truly happy to be here with you." More tears appear in Christa's eyes and roll elegantly down her face. She smiled a smile she had not ever smiled before,

"Where is the great lady who has cared for you so perfectly over all these years Leon? I wish to give her my blessings." Leon looks down and sadly shakes his head,

"She has been killed mother. In cold blood she was murdered. Thain, Thain murdered her and left her body in a stream just before he came to find me." Lady Christa stands back looking horrified and extremely surprised,

"Thain found you?" Leon again nods in agreement,

"He was very close to killing me. Shione appeared from out of nowhere and saved my life. Then we fled straight away." Lady Christa looks away,

"Thain will surely be on his way back here as we speak. This is not good for he will contact Saridus at first opportunity and that means he shall also be on his way." She looked back at Leon worryingly,

"Saridus? Meaning my father?" Christa takes Leon's head in her hands and softly runs her hands off again,

"Yes Saridus is you're farther but unfortunately Leon he has been swallowed by the wicked and hellish ways of darkness. Where as I stay pure and natural loyal to the light and wishing for hope and love, he is dark and dangerous wishing for nothing more but bloodshed and pain. I believe he can no longer be saved from what he has become. He has no love and he holds no happiness. His soul has vanished and passed away. What has been robbed from the body and once the soul has been extinguished it can never be returned. His soul is dead Leon." Leon sighs loudly,

"There are lots I wish to ask you mother but first what is this jewel and why is it so valuable to Thain?" Lady Christa turns and walks back to the cabinet and looks again in the mirror at the reflection of Leon,

"That jewel holds great power. With that jewel in your possession it makes you the most powerful man in the land. Luckily only I and now, Thain know you have it." Leon is about to reply when Shione barges through the doors,

Trilogy of Leon

"I am terribly sorry to interrupt the way I have my Lady but we need to act quickly if we are to act at all. Your plans, right now would be the ideal time to start. The men are ready and waiting." Lady Christa looks out of her window on the far wall,

"I see." Lady Christa turns to Shione,

"Let it be. Now is the right time. With so few of there soldiers in the right state to fight and so few of them being at the city anyway we have the perfect opportunity. Shione, use the royal guard. Get down to the drawbridge. At any means necessary get control of the bridge. Rid the city of the rats of darkness. Make this city ours." Shione withdraws his sword and looks at Leon,

"Are you staying here with your mother or are you going to do some work?" Leon looks at Christa,

"Leon, please help Shione and the others rid the city of the few soldiers of the dark forces. For it is freedom we wish to achieve and freedom is the heavenly way of life." Leon glances at Shione and walks over to the window where Christa was stood. He looked out at what his mother had seen. On the horizon of the far mountain he saw a force of soldiers marching toward the city. They still had a fair distance to go before they would reach the drawbridge at the moat but they were moving fast. From what Leon could see the force of soldiers was only around two thousand men. Leon turns to Shione and starts walking toward him,

"I'm going to need a sword then aren't I?" Shione laughs,

"That's the spirit lad. Quick follow me. We will find you one along the way." Leon reached the door and took a look back at his mother. As he looks at her he falls into a deep consciousness. He viewed the time of that day when he was a child looking back at this very same woman as he did now. He blinked and returned to his normal state of mind. Smiling him and Shione left the room.

5

Winning back home

They run toward the city hall and open the doors. Standing inside were a large group of well dressed ready to fight royal guard soldiers. Shione shouted out to them,

"Come on men, we have some work to do." Shione and Leon run back toward the front palace doors wit all the men from the hall following close behind with there weapons drawn. They stop at the front doors and look at each other. Shione pulls a sword from a armored statue and passed it to Leon,

"Are you ready to protect what is rightfully your home?" Leon wields the sword,

"Ready and waiting Shione." Shione holds his hand around Leon's on the handle of the sword,

"Swing hard, swing fast but be aware." They push through the doors and exit the palace confronted by another group of soldiers. Around an extra twenty to thirty soldiers stood at the steps waiting for the orders to attack. Shione points out four of the soldiers and signals them across,

"Listen up everybody. This man here is Leon. He is the Lady Christa's son. You treat him as part of the royal family and you protect him as you would the Lady. You four go with Leon. Protect him wit your lives. He is in charge of clearing the inner city grounds. Go and find all the dark soldiers. Get rid of them however you please." The four soldiers step closer to Leon waiting for him to make a move. Shione turns to Leon,

"Take these men around the city. Make sure you check every single area. Join with any other of our soldiers around the grounds and place them accordingly to search with you. All of them must be killed or disarmed. None of them must be allowed to get away." Leon looked down the steps,

"That's understood Shione but what about you?" Shione starts to walk down the steps with all of the other soldiers following him,

"Me? I'm going to go ahead to the drawbridge and make sure we get control before that small army gets any closer. Don't worry about me. Worry about yourself. I shall see you shortly." Shione continues to run down the steps and runs through the crowds with the royal guard following close behind him. Leon was left with the four guards under his command. Without saying a word he starts to walk down the steps and straight behind him the guards follow him like pets. They reach the bottom of the steps and word was going around that the great seize was taking place. Some of the city folk began to go back home while others grabbed there own swords and any available weapon at hand. Leon turns to on of the soldiers,

"Excuse me, is the whole city prepared and been waiting for this time to come?" The soldier happily replies,

"Certainly sir, we've all been planning it for some time now and everybody in the city is on Lady Christa's side. The people want nothing else but to follow the light and live happy lives sir." Leon looked carefully around. Now that people had began to filter out it became much easier to spot the soldiers from the darkness. Leon thought to himself that with the word going about of 'the seize,' that the dark soldiers would catch eye and be gathering at the front gates. Leon began running in that direction and his thoughts had proved him right. The bulk of the dark soldiers were at the front gate preventing Shione and his men making any progress toward the moat. Leon ran toward the small battle taking place and him and his four soldiers got stuck straight in with the sword on sword action. All clashing together two of the soldiers run in front of Leon covering him from a couple of sly attacks. The two other soldiers watched his back. Leon sees a chance and moved in toward one of the dark soldiers. He swung his sword toward the soldier and strikes the man's back, cutting through his flesh as if it were as soft and delicate as silk. The body of the soldier falls to the floor and the man screams in pain. A sword suddenly appears from above and crashes into the man's chest. Blood spurts out as the man's screams cease. Leon looks up and was made aware that Shione was the bearer of the sword,

"Keep focused Leon. Don't leave yourself open. Finish them off and there is no chance for them to do any more harm." The rest of the royal soldiers arrive from around the city and join with Shione and the men he was already with. Some of the soldiers instantly get engaged with fighting while Leon shouts over at Shione,

"Go Shione. Get to the moat, we shall clear here." Leon turns and runs at great speed to help one of the royal guards by slicing the neck of a dark soldier who was getting advantage of him. The soldier's neck opened up and blood sprayed through the air as Leon let the man's body fall to the ground. The body remains almost still on the ground as the blood continued to flow like a waterfall. As Leon and the soldiers helping him battle the dark soldiers at the front gate Shione and the rest of the royal guard proceed to the drawbridge. As before, there were around ten dark soldiers standing guard. The drawbridge had been opened in advance for the arrival of Thain and his men. Shione looks up at the sky,

"It won't be long until the owls come out. This is when we must be at our highest guard." The men walk calmly toward the drawbridge when the dark soldiers turn and notice there approach,

"What do you want? Go back inside the city like the rats you are." The general shouts over to them as they continue to get closer. The men begin to run at a great pace surprising the dark soldiers. In retaliation the dark soldiers withdraw there swords and become entangled in battle. As the men fight violently to the death, bodies of men fall to the muddy ground. Shione looks to his side to see a dark soldier repeatedly stabbing one of the royal guards as he lay losing his life on the ground. Shione raises his hand,

"Your not so big now are you?" The dark soldier lifted of the ground. He drops his sword as he wiggles and screams. With his power Shione launches the man into the moat after smacking him once on the ground. Shione looks quickly to the right of him to see another dark soldier running toward him with his sword held high ready to strike. Shione directed his hand at the soldier and held him still in his tracks. Not being able to move the man becomes increasingly scared. Shione walks over and embeds his sword into the man's chest. Lowering his hand the magic is cancelled and the man drops to his knees. Removing his sword Shione looks around to see that all of the dark soldiers had been killed. The moat was now secure.

Inside of the city Leon went throughout the grounds not really finding that many dark soldiers and any which they did come across were quickly and easily sorted. The soldiers with Leon spread out in different directions as Leon made his way back to the front gate with his two body guards. As he arrived Shione walked in from outside. The rest of the men that went with Shione remained at the moat standing guard. Leon and Shione step next to each other,

"All clear Leon?" Shione asked grinning,

"All clear Shione. Question, what now? The city was easily put into the hands of mother and all of us but now we have to keep it. Are we prepared for such a thing?" Shione looks away thinking to himself unconvinced that the city was ready to deal with protecting the city,

"We are ready Leon. I shall go back to the palace. We need to make arrangements for the attack force approaching us. Thain is not going to give up easily and so we need to be fully prepared." Leon looked around almost lost,

Estaban Bridges

"What shall I do Shione?" Shione laughs while walking away,

"Make yourself at home my friend because this is where you belong now. Have a look around and come back to the palace in a short while." Shione disappears through a large crowd of people in the street. The people had come from within there homes to walk amongst the streets, they were now free from darkness but yet most could not believe it. The whole city wanted to celebrate liberty but it wasn't over yet. Word had spread and just common knowledge told everybody that the city was going to become under attack. It was just the matter of a short amount of time.

The late night drew in and the moon continued to shine bright. It had been a long journey for Leon the last few days. So much had happened he tried to think clearly about it all and what could happen in the future. As he thought deeply he seemed to feel that he was to go on a long journey and meet new friends. He didn't know how right he was.

It was now the early hours of the morning and Leon had walked far around the city. Throughout his journey he met many of the city folk still around the grounds. He was not used to so many people together in one place and so close. Eventually he arrived back at the foot of the palace and walked up the long steps once again while looking over the city. Shione was waiting, sitting on the steps near the top. He had his sword in his hand and ran his hand over it. Leon looked at the sword in Shione's hand,

"That is a nice sword Shione, have you used it much?" Shione stood and replied,

"I have indeed. This sword was given to me from your mother. It was a gift because of how I defended your mother against Thain. It's almost like the connection between me and Christa." There was a short silence and Shione continued,

"Come, come, I shall show you to your room. You must be ever so tired." Leon was shown to his room and he lay down on the bed. Shione left him be and Leon closed his eyes slowly being taken away into a dream world, a dream world he was already living.

LEON, THE PEOPLE'S PERSON

Leon awoke to hear loud shouting of many people from outside the palace. He rose from his bed and dressed while listening to the deep shouts. He followed the sound through the hallways of the palace until eventually he reached the palace doors. He stood behind the as they were closed and heard the sound of his mother,

"We must not lose hope." She shouted at the top of her voice. Leon continued to open one of the doors and made his away outside. At the top of the palace steps was Lady Christa, Shione and some of the royal guard. Along all of the steps many of the city people stood and they crowded all the way down and at the bottom. Leon stood next to Shione and listened to the commotion. A middle aged man stood forward,

"My Lady, with such news of Thain and his army coming to the city, us people grow increasingly worried that we shall not be able to withstand an attack. Isn't it best that we go to the way that we were?" Lady Christa laughed ever so slightly and replied annoyed,

"You wish to go back to the life of a slave? We are all free now, we don't have to be scared and shudder at the darkness forces." A young woman emerged from the crowd beside the man who questioned before her. With a shaky scared voice she speaks out,

"My Lady, it is all well and good that we may have our freedom but for how long I ask? Can we survive the ordeal? I for one, as for many of the other mothers in the city, do not wish for any harm to come to our children." Shione reassured the woman with a soft voice,

"Dear Lady, no harm will come to your child or any other child for that matter." The crowd being unconvinced began to chant and shout once again. In there cries they shouted to surrender and give up to the oncoming army of darkness. Lady Christa became increasingly worried that her efforts were to become a waste of time. The crowd settled down and remained silent for a short moment and a small child of about ten years of age walked and knelt in front of Lady Christa. The little boy looked up whimpering and gasped, the boy puts out his hands and quietly speaks clearly,

"Lady, please don't make my mummy and daddy disappear, please. Please don't because then nobody will be there to hold my hand and sing to me at night." Lady Christa placed her hand on his head and smiled. She knelt down to his level and whispered in his ear,

"Small child, do not fear, do not worry. Nothing will happen to your mother or your father. You shall be safe and the angels of god will be there to protect us all." The

Trilogy of Leon

child jumps furiously to his feet and shouts out feeling betrayed,

"I have heard the stories of what happened to our families many years ago. The all got killed, even the little ones like me. You lie." The child turns and runs disappearing in the crowd of town folk. Lady Christa closed her eyes lowering her head and then rose to her feet. Shione looked to her and looked to Leon while shaking his head slightly. Shouting out loudly once again Lady Christa tried once again to convince her people,

"Men, woman and children, you are all my family and I care for you as I care for my own dear son. I beg of you please do not give up hope. If we stay strong, together we can get through the battle that is to come upon us. With hope and love for each other and with hope we will survive." The uproar continued and so without achievement the city folk began to turn and walk away. They began to slowly walk down the steps and disperse away from the palace. Leon saw what was happening and took it upon himself to step forward to place his word,

"People of the city, please listen, please listen to me for a short moment of your precious time." The movement ceased and one by one each of the retreating city folk turned back toward the palace opening there ears to hear what was to be said. Once Leon had got all of there attention and they had all settled he spoke out so that all could hear,

"As you all must know by now my name is Leon, I am the son of Lady Christa and I have now returned to my rightful home." A woman's voice came from the distance,

"Is that so? Then where have you been for all these years?" Leon smiled,

"I have been well taken care of by a woman so gentle and pure that with time I was brought back to Savon." Silence and so he persisted,

"Please listen to my story and I shall make a promise, my promise for your support to my mother and yourselves." With no reply he took it as a sign to continue,

"I was born in the village of Savon. I was with Lady Christa and my father in the village hall when it was attacked by Thain and his men. Thain was brutal and his men tore the village apart. My mother ran away clutching my hand, I was handed to a village woman of no royalty and we fled to a place where I would be safe. Not to long ago Thain came to this place and he murdered this woman, burnt my house and my farm. He very nearly also took my life if it was not for the good man, Shione" Leon placed his arm around Shione and Shione nodded to the people in truth of the story,

"I was brought back here and introduced to two people who have saved my life on two different occasions, my mother when I was a child and Shione when he fought Thain. Many people have lost there lives in vain. For no good reason my original fellow village folk were killed and my guardian was also killed. After all this I have not gave up. I have not given up hope, I have not given up faith and I have not given up love." He paused for a second while looking over all of the staring eyes,

"For such trauma I have survived and I continue to survive. I am here now and I know my true past. I am willing to fight for the future. I am willing to give my life for those around me, for hope, love and faith. My plea to

Trilogy of Leon

you as my fellow city folk is to go into battle against Thain when he arrives with his men. I shall be the first to leave the city gates and I shall be the last to reenter them once we are victorious in battle. In return for my proof of my loyalty I just ask of you, I beg you, do not fall and hide but stand tall and together. Stand strong and do not be afraid. Have hope for the future. Have faith for the reasons we fight and have the love which we so badly deserve. I do not wish to see any more of the people who are of my past; present and future fall to death or to darkness. Please unite with us. Fight with us. Survive with us." A silent dreamy minute passed over the city. Nobody so much as blinked but thought about the speech that Leon had just laid out to them. Breaking the silence a large man, a butcher of the city, walked up to Leon at the top of the steps. The butcher put out his hand and shook Leon's with his full respect. The man lifts his head slightly and took a deep breath,

"It would be a great honor to fight for what is right. It would be well within my duty as a man of this city to fight for her Lady and for the rest of the people. I grant you my hands in battle Leon. You inspire the deepest of my feelings." The butcher bowed his head at Lady Christa and stood alongside Leon. Looking over the rest of the people each one looked at each other. Within the crowd near the back a voice shouted,

"Hope, faith, love." Another voice repeated and then another and so forth. Eventually the entire crowd was shouting those words. Lady Christa smiled in delight, as did Shione and Leon.

From then the city became entranced and grouped together as close as any community could possibly be.

Preparations became under way to equip all those who needed armor and weaponry. Lady Christa took a chance to thank Leon for his great words and Leon took them to heart. Leon was equipped with the best weapons of Shione and the best armor he could find. It was not going to be long before Thain and his men would arrive at the city moat.

Throughout the day and going into the night the city rustled with commotion. The sky was clear and the stars glittered there greatness over the land. The people of the city were fast asleep after along day of excitement, anxiousness and busyness. Lady Christa, Leon and Lord Shione sat in the throne room talking amongst themselves about the past and what was to happen with the fight against Thain. Lady Christa spoke freely,

"You are very much right Shione, tomorrow will be the day that Thain will arrive. As planned I shall stay somewhere behind the city walls giving what help I can from inside. With my power I will be able to rock them from there feet and Shione, if you can raise the winds to disturb them it would be of great help. All of the royal guard will be first to leave the city gates and then the city folk who have joined the city force. Leon, you can remain inside of the city walls with me." Leon huffed and shook his head,

"I am sorry mother but you seem to be mistaken. I said to the city folk that I shall be the first out and the last in, I plan to keep to my word and honor my promise." Lady Christa thought quickly to herself about the thought of Leon getting injured,

"But Leon, I do not wish for you to be hurt." Leon stood his ground,

Trilogy of Leon

"I am keeping to my word." The night went on and the three of them went to sleep in there chambers. Each with there own dreams, dreams only to true.

DEFENDING FREEDOM

The sun appeared and the city came to life. It was a clear warm day. It was said that it was a perfect day for a victorious battle against the darkness. Shione pushed through the door to Leon's chamber awakening him from a deep sleep. Somewhat excited Shione seemed to bounce around the room picking up Leon's cloths and throwing them at him. He shouted loudly to wake Leon up more clearly,

"Come on Leon, they are here. It's time." Shione ran out of the chamber and Leon listened as Shione ran down the hallway screaming,

"I'm going to get you; I'm going to get you good." This was followed by a draining laughter as Shione got out of range. Leon quickly got dressed and put on his armor. Leaning against the side of the bed was a large sword. It was built to the highest of standards and it was as sharp as the sharpest teeth of a shark. Lady Christa walked in to find Leon standing wielding his sword and practicing moves. He did not notice she had arrived so she creped up on him quietly and whispered gently,

"You must have learnt that of your father. He was always good with a sword." Leon spun around and lowered his sword feeling slightly embarrassed, in reply he laughed,

"I haven't learnt anything from my father. If I had, I would have killed myself already." Leon stepped around Lady Christa and began to move toward the door, he took a look back,

"Mother, we shall win this battle. I can assure you." Christa smiled still worried for his safety,

"Take care and watch every possible angle Leon."

Leon approached the front gate moving between the gathered royal guards and city men. As he approached all fell silent apart from a distant sound of chanting from Thain's men. As Leon walked through all of the men he was tapped on the back many times. He stood next to Shione, who was ready and waiting,

"The men respect you Leon. They honor you." Shione said checking Leon's armor to see if it was fitted properly, Leon replied,

"But why Shione? What have I done to deserve such high regards?" Shione slapped him slightly on the face,

"Wake up Leon; you have turned these people around. I must add I was maybe also giving up hope until your little speech yesterday. You are an idol to these people Leon. Ready to fight what is right and stand up against the darkness. You are a loved man." Leon seemed to blush as one of the soldiers approached with Savior. The soldier passed Leon the reigns and shook his hand saying,

Trilogy of Leon

"My Lord, May the god of Light be with you. All of us will be." The soldier ran off into line and Leon looked back at Shione,

"Lord?" He questioned. Shione pointed at Leon with one finger,

"A loved man Leon, a loved man." Leon took it in his stride and ran his hand gently over Saviors neck. He spoke quietly,

"Keep me safe old friend. I beg you, keep me safe once again." Savoir neighed as if he understood and Leon climbed onto his back. Shione joined by his side on the back of his horse. Shione explained the attack plan to Leon,

"When the gates open they won't expect to see all of us. They will expect to see us on our knees. Lady Christa wall use her magic to unsettle them slightly and then I shall use my own magic to unsettle them further. They will no doubt not be able to cross the moat until Thain makes them a path. Once this has happened we ride out and, well, hope for the best." Leon looked behind at all of the soldiers staring ahead at him and Shione,

"Understood Shione, understood. We won't fail." Shione once again patted Leon on the shoulder,

"We won't fail because we all have hope, faith and love Leon." He paused and faced forward looking at the gates. He looked back slightly once more as the gates began to open,

"Face it Leon, you were born a hero."

As the gates became fully open Leon and Shione were left with a dangerous view. Thain sat upon his horse in front of a good two thousand soldiers. It was all silent across the city and across the land of Savon. Not one

Estaban Bridges

bird sang and not one leaf shuffled. It was a nervous atmosphere. Thain looks with evilness in his eye, across the moat surprised to see two men on horseback. After a few moments he realizes it was Lord Shione and Leon. He cursed to himself at became angered. Thain signaled one of his generals and spoke with an infuriated tone,

"Get this bridge down as quick as you can. We have a battle to start." The general got some of the soldiers and they fired roped spikes at the bridge as so they could pull the bridge down with all of there force. Lady Christa watched hiding behind the city walls. She raised her hand and closed her eyes. Quietly she muttered,

"Earth, land, lend me your strength. Rumble the ground with your full anger. Send the evil to there hand's and knees." A bright light flashed around her and as asked the land began to shake. Violently the shaking concentrated on the other side of the moat. Thain's soldiers began to shuffle and become ungrouped as the power of the magic made some fall to the floor. Thain's horse became reckless and began to step randomly. Thain growled,

"Mere witches magic." Shione went ahead to mutter as he raised his hand,

"The wind that governs the clouds in the sky, release your fury. Twirl the evil, shake the evil. Throw the evil." Once again the power Shione possessed showed its might. A small gust of wind began to blow amongst Thain and his army as well as the shaking of the earth. The earthquake became even more unsteady cracking under the army's feet. More soldiers fell and others became shaken. The wind picked up and blew some of the soldiers into others sending them crashing to the floor. Some of the soldiers got spun around and made dizzy as others got cold in the

Trilogy of Leon

strong breeze. Thain became overwhelmed with rage as the drawbridge was finally pulled down. Shione looked at Leon and Leon knew what he had to do. He began to trot forward on Savior and he left the city gates. Close behind Shione followed. Behind them the royal guard marched forward toward the battle field. Thain charged over the bridge with his men pouring in after him. Time seemed to be slow and muffled as the two groups, one evil, one good approached each other. The two sides galloped across the empty ground ready to clash. Time went from slow to quick as the battle began. Swords sliced across chests and across faces. Arms were detached and legs severed from the bodies of soldiers. Leon fought hard, watching everyway possible he stabbed and cut at the dark soldiers. Body after body fell to the ground as blood stained and gushed everywhere. Savior moved protecting certain possible vital blows as Leon continued to chop the soldiers down. The coat of Saviors body became drenched in blood. Hardly any of his white coat could be seen through all of the blood. Shione fought many of the soldiers at one time, with so with ease. Thain hunted his way through the royal guard as if it were nothing but sport. His confidence proved to be too high when he was knocked from his horse. On the ground he defended against many of the royal guard trying to cut his head from his body. They would have liked to see nothing else but his blood spilt like the blood of all the innocents he had killed in cold blood. After a short time the rest of the soldiers from within the city walls charged out to join and help the others. At the front of these soldiers was the butcher. He did not wield a sword but a large butcher's knife in each hand. The majority of the city men were

Estaban Bridges

in this second attack force as the woman and children remained in the city praying for there safe return. These soldiers engaged in the battle and Thain looked around the battle to see that he had underestimated his opponent. He began to feel less confident about the situation. As he looked about defending himself with great power he caught a glimpse of Shione standing on the ground. Thain made his way through the bleeding bodies and fighting soldiers toward him. With Shione's back turned toward Thain he fought three dark soldiers. Thain lifted his sword up high. Ready to strike he grins to himself about what small victory that this death would give him. Thain began to lower his sword with all his power as Shione turned to see the blade coming toward him. Suddenly Leon on the back of Savior rushed behind Thain and Leon's sword cut along his back from right to left. Thain dropped to his knees as Leon came back around. Shione stumbled backward dazed by the ordeal. Leon rode toward Thain to give him a final blow but as he got close amazingly Thain rolled out of harms way and struck Leon with a coil of lightning. With the shock of the attack Leon fell from Savior to the ground and shook slightly. Thain lifted his sword to try and get his final blow on Leon but his attempt was foiled. Savior had turned around quickly and lifted onto his back to legs. In the air he lashed out with his hooves and scared Thain away. Shione moved in to attack and swung his sword getting occupied with Thain. Leon was able to recover quickly from his quick shock and jumped back onto Savior, immediately he was in action again taking on more dark soldiers. Knowing he was soon to be defeated Thain fled away from Shione; he gave chase but was interacted by more of the dark soldiers.

Trilogy of Leon

Thain made his way back to the drawbridge and looked around. Without many of his own soldiers left he called the retreat. With this the darkness soldiers that were left ran to escape. Upon retreat more were killed. One was running away from the butcher and so he chucked one of his knives which imbedded into his back. The butcher ran straight over and jumped onto him cutting him up with his other knife. Shione and Leon stood not being approached by any more soldiers and watched as Thain and a few hundred managed to scramble away. Leon galloped over to Shione's side,

"We've won, there fleeing." Shione looks up at Leon and replied with a tired voice,

"We haven't won anything Leon. He will be back again." Leon's feeling of success became drained away. He looked around to see that many of the city folk and many of the royal guard had survived. Leon shouted down to Shione,

"Lets go, lets give chase. We can get Thain and finish this." Shione stood silent and shook his head. Remaining silent he turned and began to step back toward the city. Leon followed by his side,

"Why not Shione? We can finish this?" Shione looked up to the sky and wiped his face with his hand,

"Too many men have lost there lives for one sunny day Leon. It's best we take care of the wounded." With this Shione continued to walk and came across a dark soldier still half alive. He looked down at him and the man cried out in pain, the soldier grabbed hold of his leg and begged for mercy, he said,

"Please, help me, please?" Shione breathed deeply and lifted his sword. With one quick hard blow he cut the man's head straight from his neck. The body shuddered and the head rolled along the floor. Shione spoke down to the corpse,

"The innocent people you have murdered were not given help. My help to you is I saved you from yourself, from darkness."

The day moved on slowly. The injured were taken into the city and treated for there wounds they had sustained. Shione disappeared for a short while having some time to clear his mind. Leon helped with the injured as Lady Christa walked among them looking at the pain of the city folk. The battle field outside the city was cleaned of innocent life and bodies but the dark soldiers remained lying in there own blood. They were stripped of there weapons and were left. Rain had begun to set itself down on the land washing away blood of the wounded and the dead. The dead were mourned after and they were given there blessings by a man of god. There souls were laid to rest and there bodies quickly buried.

THE RETURN OF THAIN

Around mid afternoon Shione sat in the palace with Lady Christa and Leon. No conversation was held but each of them were in there own deep thought. A loud knock beckoned the doors to the room and a royal guard stepped in,

"I am terribly sorry to bother you. Please forgive me but I have some potentially bad news." Lady Christa looked over at the guard and replied quietly,

"It is quite alright, please continue." The guard removed his helmet and held it to his side,

"Thain has returned. He sits with what's left of his army outside of the moat my Lady. They wait quietly and seem to be, quite relaxed." Shione looks over at Lady Christa to see her reaction. She looks to him giving the expression for his advice,

"We can't ask them to go back out again my Lady. Not twice in the same day. We have all seen far too much fighting than we wish." Lady Christa questioned,

Estaban Bridges

"What if he is waiting for reinforcements?" Leon steps in,

"We can take care of Thain and his few hundred men tomorrow, most of them are injured and so we shouldn't have too much trouble." Christa takes the opinions and looks back at the guard,

"Do not worry. Tell all they do not have to go back into battle today but keep aware." The soldier bows and leaves closing the door behind him.

The day went further on and the city remained in a cold atmosphere of death and sorrow. All thought what was to happen in the next day but yet all still held hope and faith in what was to happen and what it would happen for. Love was still strong throughout the city so all was calm although quiet.

Early in the morning, around four, a figure moved through the shadows of the great city walls. Wearing a full hooded cloak the figure reaches the city gates. The figure stands hesitating and then lays a knock upon the gates. A small hatch in the door is opened by a guard and a pair of eyes peers through at the figure in the darkness. The guard speaks through the gates,

"What business do you have here?" the man waits for a reply and the figure moves close to the small hatch and peers through looking directly into the eyes of the guard,

"I must see the Lady at once for I have some important information she would need to hear." The guard's eyes move from the hatch and look away. They return toward the figure,

"How did you get over the moat and past Thain's army for there is not a passage across?"

Trilogy of Leon

The figures head shakes slowly and laughter comes from under the hood,

"It is a moat my friend, in a moat there is water and to get over water all I needed was a small coracle. Is that so hard to believe?" The guard questions again,

"And Thain's army?" The figure moves slightly away from the hatch in the gates,

"One person can move quickly and quietly through sleeping danger." The eyes behind the gates move away out of sight and the sound of locks being undone could be hurt. A small doorway opened in one of the gates and the figure moved in through the entrance with the door being closed behind him and locked again the figure lowers his hood. The cloaked man looks about to see that this guard was the only one on duty other than one asleep a few yards away. The man looks at the guard as the guard looks at him puzzled,

"Don't you believe that there is a few to many reckless people in this world my friend, including yourself and me?" The guard takes a step back,

"Thain?" The guard withdraws his sword and defends himself against the possible threat.

Loudly the guard screams,

"Thain, Thain is here." A lion's head of pure flame burnt from the palm of Thain's hand.

He fires the flame like a striking bolt. As the lions head drifts quickly toward the guard its jaw opens wide and then it hits, bites, it clings onto the guard's throat, biting through his soft flesh. His skin burning as it's penetrated. The guard's screams turn to squeaks as his body falls to the floor with a thump. From behind the second guard had awoke and swung his sword at Thain's

Estaban Bridges

back but without hesitation Thain withdraws his own sword and sinks it into his chest as he ran toward him. With all the commotion a street dweller had ran to fetch reinforcements to battle against the intruder. Thain proceeded through the darkness of the streets quietly and quickly. He kneels on one knee in the shadows and closes his eyes with one hands fingers touching softly against the earth. He receives a vision of Leon further in the city at a water fountain sitting looking at the jewel in his hand. Thain revives from the vision and knowing exactly Leon's position he continues through the street. Thain walks out of the shadows looking at Leon sitting upon the side of the fountain. As he had seen Leon was holding the jewel in his hand looking at it in deep thought. Thain speaks out quietly to Leon,

"I believe it is you who they now call Leon." Leon looks up. Shocked by the presence of

Thain he leaps to his feet instantly grasping for his sword and withdrawing it to an offensive stance.

"And you are Thain. You desecrated my home and murdered my guardian. You persist to reek hell upon me and the people" Thain smiles and wields his sword,

"Please Leon, enough of the compliments. I've come to retrieve what is rightfully mine." Leon holds his sword up pointing it toward Thain,

"I am not scared of you and neither are the people within these walls. Fight me. I beg you." Gladly excepting the invitation Thain sprints toward Leon. There swords clash like strikes of lightning. The battle emerges hard and fast. Violently stabbing and swinging they run circles around each other. They get stuck in a stand off at swords end walking around constantly. The world seemed to

Trilogy of Leon

wrap around them as they stared into each others eyes. They both saw the hatred towards each other in the looks of there eyes. They both fight wanting each other bleeding and begging for mercy. As they continue to pursue in there tiring exchange of hammering blows a couple of soldiers are drawn into the fight.

Before they intrude they advice another soldier to warn others and summon Lady Christa and Lord Shione. As that soldier did as was told the others moved to help Leon. But as they get a few yards close to Thain they are blocked by spiraling spikes from the ground shooting up at them pushing them further and further away from where the two fearless swordsmen were fighting. The world now watches them interact with force. The look of persistence on there faces to win and be victorious. With both men equal in power and force they slightly lower there swords and then plunge into each other. All goes quiet.

They stand there holding each other up with both of them having one hand still holding each of the swords. After a few moments of timeless agony the two men separate. They stutter backward a few steps pulling the swords from inside one another. The swords dripped with the blood of them both. On Leon's sword was the blood of an almighty dark force leader and on Thain's sword the blood of a hero. Leon lets go slowly of the grasp around the sword he held and it fell to the floor. The sword landed, no longer to be used again by the hand of Leon. Thain holds to his entry wound while looking at Leon. Still

looking into each others eyes Leon's takes steps towards the man faced before him and rests his head on his shoulder. Leon turns and whispers into Thain's ear quietly,

"For the deaths of so many I give you pain." Leon thrushes a small dagger he had got from his belt into Thain's Chest. He twists it while pushing in harder and deeper into

Thain's chest as he lets out a roar of pain and hurt. Thain pushes Leon away. With the force Leon's falls to the ground with blood clearly visible on his hand and stained into his cloths. Thain walks over and places his sword to Leon's throat,

"I am glad I get to see you die." After a pause of Leon looking up at him from below

Thain drives his sword into the chest of Leon and withdraws it. Leaning on his sword he kneels down,

"The jewel is mine now." As Thain reaches for the jewel he is struck through his arm with an arrow. He rises to his feet looking out for who had shot at him. Standing there was Lord Shione and Lady Christa with a large handful of men. Knowing he was severely injured Thain begins to flee away from the scene. Lord Shione and his men give chase after Thain who ran back the way he came. From the distance they headed screams of pain could be heard as Thain defended himself with magic against the soldiers. The sound of burning and mild destruction could also be heard as Shione and Thain battled.

Meanwhile Lady Christa went to her son's side. She held him close.

9

Hopes death

Leon looked into the eyes of his mother as he lay there in her arms. Her eyes connected with his with an extreme power of love. Tears roll from her eyes. The tears full of sorrow and sadness at the thought of the death of her son. Leon lye's before her bleeding. His warm blood staining his cloths as it leaks from his wound,

"I, I don't want to die" Leon coughs violently still looking at his mothers eyes. Leon continues,

"What is life? I believe life is just a lie" Lady Christa holds her hand to Leon's cheek.

With her the smoothness of her thumb she wipes away Leon's tears of disbelieve,

"All I have ever really known is the curse of death and now I am the one who is to die. I don't want to die. I don't, I don't want to be forgotten" Leon looks away in shame from his mother. Soldiers crowd around Leon and Lady Christa as well as people of the city, they look at Leon, the man who they admire. They stand shocked looking at Leon and Lady Christa lying there together. They all stand silent and motionless. All of them wished they could do something or say something to help. Shione pushes through the crowd and walks to where Leon lay with Lady Christa clutching him, holding onto him.

She felt like she was holding onto his life. Shione kneels down beside Lady Christa and places his hand upon her shoulder. She looks up at him wanting to gain some sort of a miracle, some way of saving her son. Shione shakes his head and whispers to Lady

Christa,

"I am sorry my Lady. He got away through the front gates. I couldn't get through the power he used against me. I wish I was able to catch him for I would love to rip his heart from within him and bring it to you on my knees." Lady Christa looks back down at Leon,

"Leon, my son, you will never be forgotten. We will remember you for all of time. We will sing your name and a giant statue shall be built of you in the centre of the city. We will praise you and love you but you have to be there" More tears trickle down her cheek.

Leon manages a small happy smile,

"In life, I love you. In death, I will wait for you" Leon slowly reaches for his mothers hands on his face and pulls it down to his chest, with strong words and from the heart he whispers,

"Mother, I love you" upon this his tight hold of Lady Christa's hand loosens and his eyes slowly close. His head falls back gently and his body becomes drained. Death had found him and god had taken him.

Lady Christa lays Leon's body on the ground and through the tears and the heartache, the pain and the

Trilogy of Leon

sorrow she kisses him softly on his forehead. She stands up tall and strong. She turns to Shione and places her hand on his shoulder and looks up into his eyes. She had the look of anger and hatred. With a voice of power and revenge she announces to Shione, the Soldiers and the people of the city,

"We shall fight. No more hiding. We shall go to them. Vengeance, Vengeance shall be ours and we will be free." As she walks toward the crowd of people they make way for her to pass. She walks heading toward the palace.

Shione is left looking down at Leon's once so strong and active body. He kneels down and starts to pick him up to put him over his shoulders. Some of the soldiers standing in the crowd walk over and help Shione with raising Leon's body from the ground. They all march slowly behind each other through the city toward the palace.

Along the way the March gains soldiers from the streets and city folk also join. All was silent. Nobody spoke and there was not a sound apart from the wind blowing slightly and the sound of all the steps of the people. Some of the followers were crying and others looked at the ground in sadness. Was this man being carried before them, there hope, now dead? More people from windows above along the streets of the city let petals fall to the ground over the march. The atmosphere was cold and the one death seemed as if it had been the death of so many. Leon was there courage. A man who had lost near to

everything stayed so strong and fought for what was right. Now he was dead they had lost most of there hope, there inspiration. Eventually the march reached the palace.

Shione carried Leon's body alone in his arms up the many steps. Everybody else remained at the foot of the steps looking up at Shione traveling the stairs. When Shione reached the top of the steps he turns and bows his head. He closes his eyes and whispers a prayer. He looks back up to find the people below had knelt and also bowed there heads in respect and love. Leon's pride would last forever in the hearts of the people and threw the generations. As the people remained knelt Shione enters the palace and walks to Leon's room. He places Leon's body on his bed and moves his hands over each other on his chest. He looks down at Leon and smiles while touching Leon's hand with his,

"Time to get them brother, time to be set free." Shione leaves the room closing the doors behind him. He strides quickly to Lady Christa's room. On arrival he knocks loudly and enters without waiting for permission. He is faced with Lady Christa in a long dress. It was black all other and the skirt became torn along the length of her right leg. She turns to Shione,

"Shione, as you know it is time, time to banish them. We will reclaim this land. The fight will start here and spread all over. I will fight until my very own last breath." Lady

Christa walks over to the wall and removes an old staff. Engraved onto it was a snake from the bottom its tail and it went to its head at the top. The snakes head had its mouth wide open but nothing came from inside. She again looks at Shione,

Trilogy of Leon

"This was a present from Thain to Saridus for joining the dark forces. This was the weapon Thain used to destroy the original village of Savon. What Saridus didn't realize was Thain kept it here so it would not be stolen or lost. All Thain needed was my jewel.

Now I can get it back" She walks toward the door. Shione mentions,

"I lay Leon in his room my Lady. May I ask, what does the jewel do?" lady Christa looks at the staff she held,

"With the jewel placed in the snake's mouth it becomes activated. It's the power of the elements and the gods themselves. The jewel Leon has right now has all the four elements combined and throughout the world there is a jewel representing each element. The jewel Leon has is the most powerful." Shione shakes his head not quite understanding Lady Christa's explanation,

"The purpose of the jewel is to banish all evil and save the innocent" Lady Christa walks quickly to Leon's room with Shione close behind. Standing next to Leon's body on the bed Lady Christa removes the jewel from around his neck. She kisses his forehead softly and brushes her hand through his hair,

"Thank you for taking care of this for me Leon." She turns and lowers the staff. Carefully she places the jewel comfortably into the mouth of the engraved snake. Magically the eyes of the snake light up red. As it does so a revolving whirl of magic emerges. A small spike of earth rose from the middle with a little wall of flame around it. Around that just above the flame was a ring of water. The water and ring of flame was being revolved with the power of wind. Lady Christa holds the staff up straight, smiles and looks at

Shione,

"The power of Earth, Air, Fire and Water. The four elements keep the world together. With the four elements making life whoever holds this and controls this becomes a god. One the one side I have fire and water. This makes complete light. Pure and true light. We call this Holy and on the other side air and earth. Full destructive power, power of darkness."

Shione stands silent looking amazed at Lady Christa,

"So Lady Christa, you are a goddess." He kneels bowing his head. Lady Christa smiles,

"Raise Shione, with this, the ultimate weapon, we have hope, we have a chance. We can make a difference now. Lets not waste valuable time." Shione stands and withdraws his sword,

"Then let's go my Lady. Let the battle begin." With this Lady Christa and Shione walk out of the room closing the doors behind them and walk toward the entrance of the palace. Both of them ready to fight. Both of them ready to do what is necessary. Both of them ready to die for what they believe in.

They reach the palace doors and leave. Standing at the top of the steps they look down. They see the streets full of all the soldiers and all of the people who lived in the city. They had all been waiting in suspense to find out what was to happen and what was to be done. Lady Christa stands forward and lifts the staff for all to see,

"My friends of the city, if you have no hope, then that will soon change. Here in my hand

I have the ultimate weapon. The weapon to save us from darkness. It is time for us to stand now. It is time

Trilogy of Leon

for us to fight" The crowd remains silent as Lady Christa looks down at them and lowers the staff. She looks at Shione but Shione says nothing. A man from the crowd steps forward and walks up a few steps so that he can be heard,

"I do not wish to offend or really question you my Lady but how can we believe that about the weapon?" Lady Christa thinks for a second on what to do. She looks at the staff and raises it high,

"The light and the dark, the sun and the moon. Cross now in your paths and blind the earth" suddenly the sky starts to darken from the early morning light. The people look up at the sun and see that the moon began to cover it. It covers the sun with a solar eclipse and from all around gasps of shock and amazement can be heard. The moon and separates from its path in front of the sun and the earth is once again introduced to light. Lady Christa starts to walk down the steps,

"Who will join in the fight for freedom? Who will join in the fight for survival?" She shouts to them all. Random people from the crowd step forward and eventually the hole crowd begins to cheer and volunteer to fight for there city and for the freedom of them all. Shione takes it upon himself to organize the people with jobs and responsibilities. He made sure that all the men able to fight were equipped with a weapon. He got teenage children supplying the bowman on the city walls with arrows. He organized for the woman to help take care of anyone who would be injured and to take care of the children.

10
REVENGE FOR A LOVED ONE.

A few hours later after all the excitement everybody was in position and waiting to begin. People were scared and anxious but ready to do what was necessary to protect there futures. Lady Christa stood at the front gates with Shione. In front of them, stood the elite guards of the Palace and City. Behind them were soldiers. Lady Christa sat upon a horse, the horse of Leon's, Saviour. Lord Shione was also upon his horse. Lady Christa addresses the people,

"My soldiers and my protectors. May we battle long and hard. May the gods be with you.

When the gates open we will have the element of surprise." Shione continues after her,

"We shall charge toward the drawbridge. We will attack on there side of the moat over the bridge, which Thain has still got lowered. We shall not back down until every one of them has been laid to rest." The soldiers all nodded understanding the plan and wielded there

Estaban Bridges

weapons. Lady Christa says the final words before the battle,

"I shall be fighting for us all and for all our freedom." Lord Shione raises his sword and the gates are opened. The view in front of them seemed to drag as if it were an endless road. They start to march forward leaving the safety of the city. Shouting could be heard from across the bridge as Thain and his army realized that they were soon to be attacked.

They begin to scramble to there feet to get prepared for the confrontation.

The bowman on top of the city walls open fire trying to reach over the moat but with no such luck they cease to waste the arrows. Lady Christa notices that the bowman were having no such luck and points the staff forward to where they were heading,

"Gods of power hear my words. Listen to my prayer and please lend me your power. May the winds carry our arrows with the speed of lightning and may they strike the enemy with the crash of thunder." After a short pause Lady Christa looked up to the sky. Sure enough a light gust of wind blows. The light wind turns stronger. It grows so high that the clouds above begin to slide across the sky. Lord Shione turns and faces the city. He shouts at the highest of his voice,

"Fire the arrows. Fire them now." The bowman take a second chance at firing there arrows over the moat and the arrows drift far from where they had before. They cross the moat at a high speed and launch themselves into the enemy soldiers. They continue the attack as they army of freedom fighters charge forward. As they reach the bridge the first wave of Thain's soldiers charge across to

Trilogy of Leon

interact with the approaching forces. The two forces clash violently and bodies of stabbed victims fall to the floor. With such a tight space men fall of the sides and into the moat but after a short time the space is cleared leaving room for Shione to lead his men over. Shione crosses on horse back slaying men running toward him and his men follow close slaying others. They all reach the other side apart from Lady Christa and a few of her protectors. Lady Christa watches to see how she can help. The bowman cease fire and leave there stations on the city walls and also take up arms. They leave the city gates to help with the struggle over the city moat. Lady

Christa looks across the large stretch of land to see a large army of men running toward the battle to join Thain's side. The leader of the army was none other than Saridus himself. She raises her staff once more and speaks to the gods,

"May one now become punished for his temptation of the past. Will the god of the earth sacrifice his power to condemn evil? Please save Saridus from the hell within his heart."

The staff lights up and the spike of stone rose a little higher in length. Lady Christa looks over at the advancing army. She is surprised to see a large spike of rock and stone emerge from the ground. Saridus on his horse plunge straight toward it and the spike shoots threw his body shearing his body in two. His body pieces fall to the ground as his horse runs away. The army riding behind him halts and they all stand amazed at the great magic they had just witnessed. Out of fear for there lives they turn and flee away from the battle scene, leaving Thain and his men alone to fight the attack.

Estaban Bridges

As the rest of the men run across toward the bridge to cross the moat Thain appears from the other side. The reinforcements begin to cross wielding there weapons but as they get halfway Thain raises his hand collapsing the bridge into the moat making the men fall. As they try to swim to either side of the moat Lady Christa watches to see

Thain again raise his hand. A large glowing magma ball of earth rises from the ground and he launches it toward the moat. Upon impact it would instantly kill all of the men swimming to safety. Lady Christa reacts quickly and summons a new spell,

"Water of the moat, protect the innocent within against the wrath of the evil." Suddenly

the water of the moat raises and the men swimming drop to the floor as the water raises above there heads producing a protective roof which casts away the magma fire ball thrown toward them. Thain looks up at Lady Christa and a dominant smile is given.

Thain walks to the edge of the moat and produces a single walk way with the power of the earth and protects himself as he walks across in a large fire ball. As he reaches the other side Lady Christa's men move to protect her but deem no match for his explosive fire ball shield which he erupts from around him. Left standing there alone was Thain and Lady Christa herself, Thain shouts over the commotion of the battle taking place,

"Lady Christa. I do admire your courage but your stupidity is the same as your sons."

Lady Christa dismounts from the Saviour horse,

Trilogy of Leon

"Thain, you have plagued my people for to long. Now you will suffer all at once the suffering you have caused others." Thain laughs loudly,

"You, you shall be the one to suffer" He clutches his fist and a wall of flame surrounds them both. Thain raises his horse and runs toward Lady Christa swinging uncontrollably as she defends with the staff. He growls as he attacks her,

"The staff, the power will all be mine." He knocks her to the floor and raises his sword up high in preparation to drive it threw her body. As if in slow motion as he lowers the sword a blade appears from his chest. It dripped with blood as he let go of his sword and he fell to the ground. Standing there in front of Lady Christa and Thain was Lord Shione.

He puts out his hand and helps Lady Christa to her feet. Shione looks at her and smiles,

"Even with the power of the gods you still need my help my Lady." They are interrupted when Thain rises to his feet,

"It is not over yet" Thain fires a spike of burning scorching heat and knocks Shione a good few feet from where he was standing and turns to attack Lady Christa once again.

Without a chance he is lifted from the ground by a gust of wind and held unsuspended. A slow spiral of earth wrapped around his body holding him tightly. Next a small bright flame begins to rise along the spiral and bursts his body into flames. As he is held trapped his body burns,

"Now you feel the pain of those you have tortured" Lady Christa turns and walks away toward Shione to see if he was injured. Across the moat the forces of darkness had been slain and those who had left had managed to flee. The men still alive stood tall over the dead and began to cheer in the glee of victory. Shione rises to his feet and Lady Christa looks over at the burning corpse of Thain,

"This is just the beginning Shione. We have much more to accomplish." As they begin to walk back to the city the rest of the men cross the single passage bridge over the moat to join them. They pass Thain's fateful state and Lady Christa turns, looks at his body still burning. She smile and clicks her fingers. A large amount of cool water splashes over his leaving him steaming. They return to the palace including the men from who were in the moat.

11

THE EYE OF THE STORM.

A few weeks pass. The city becomes full of love and care. There was not a drop of darkness left within the city or the surrounding area. Lady Christa had sent Lord

Shione and his men after the darkness forces that had got away and to spread the word that the land was now free. As Lady Christa had promised a statue was made of Leon and it was placed at the foot of the city palace. At the bottom it read 'not one will be forgotten but all will be remembered. Legends have left but legends live on.'

For now, the land of Savon was at peace and liberty ruled all over. The city folk of the city of Savon continued to live there lives the best they could but Lady Christa knew in her heart that the war was not over. The war had only just begun.

Great within the depths of a large city covered by black clouds a man with a helmet shaped like a dragons head growls angrily while looking across the city. A woman steps up beside him draping her arms over his shoulders. She whispers into his ear gently,

"The hero was slain by Thain master. You have no need to worry." The man shakes the woman off him and looks at her from within the helmet,

"Christa has much power. This is what I worry."

With the death of Leon only one thing was certain, a hero dead needs to be a hero replaced. What if the hero is revived? Further future will be laid out in, Hero Reborn.

Part 2

Hero Reborn

A Soul Worth Returning

Hero Reborn
A soul worth returning

Is a lost soul a lost course? Should a soul be returned to a body or is this against the nature of life itself? Is a life not worth living, an unworthy life? The main focus is that once a person dies, the soul lives on and if the soul can be passed on for the good of humanity and for the good of life, then maybe it is right to return this soul to earth. If a soul is returned to earth and put into a new life form, is this life form secure or is it unstable and open to breakdown? It is only time that can tell.

It's been six months since the extraordinary battle between light and darkness. Six months since the death of the hero, Leon. All has been quiet and all has been calm but this is unsettling for the people who live in fear against the darkness. The quietness only points to one option and that is that the darkness are building up there forces and making a strategy which will be so great and so powerful that the people who fight for hope and love will be crushed and there lives demolished through one big offensive attack. Lady Christa summons her only daughter who has great power passed down through generations. With the power combined there may just be hope. There may just be survival for what matters the most, innocent and cherished life worth living.

The moon hides behind large clouds in the dark sky. Stars twinkle and flash beautifully. The atmosphere calm and all is quiet A lone rider strolls slowly over empty land upon a glittering black horse with hair so shiny it reflected a small glow when the moon caught at the right angle. The stranger moves ever more closely to the new found city of light, the city of Savon. From the city gates appears Lady Christa, the queen of the rebellion, the queen of the new hope against the darkness. She rode upon a well built horse. The horse named Savior. By her side was Lord Shione the queen's personnel body guard and high general. Lady Christa and Lord Shione ride to the moat bridge and wait in anticipation as it slowly lowers. The stranger waits patiently on the other side. As the bridge comes to a halt lowered fully, the stranger proceeds to cross and as she does so she removes her hood. Revealed from hiding is a beautiful face of a young woman. Skin so smooth it was as smooth as the softest of silk. Skin so clean it was clearer than the clearest sky. Her bright blue eyes full of innocents. Blond hair came down across her face and blows gently in the wind. The magnificent perfect young woman smiles and halts just in front of Lady Christa and Shione,

"It's nice to see you mother and you to Shione." Lady Christa smiles the biggest of all smiles,

"I hope your trip was not to exhausting my daughter and how nice it is to see you. I'm so glad you're good and well." Shione also smile and bows his head,

"Greetings Lady Catherine, it has been a long time." The three of them began to ride slowly back toward the city from the moat. Lady Catherine speaks of her journeys as Shione and Lady Christa listen intrigued by the stories of fine battles and legendary warriors. As they enter the city through the gates Lady Christa turns and places her hand onto Lady Catherine's,

"My child, I'm glad you answered my summoning. Your brother I always spoke of returned to me thanks to Shione but misfortune passed our way. Your brother was slain in battle with Lord Thain. I hope with your power and mine we might be able to return him once more to this world." With a small grin Lady Catherine replies,

"My brother and your sons' body will never be able to return mother but the soul can be passed to the greater body of an immortal with the power we possess." Shione continuing ahead turns his head back to look at where the royal Ladies were,

"My ladies, we can surely discuss this further and more comfortably in the palace. For it is ever so cold and I would like to sit by the fire." Breaking up the serious atmosphere they laugh and continue to the palace.

Within the palace the three of them sit close to a small but fierce fire, burning and crackling providing warmth. They all began explaining to each other how the past had come about. Lady Catherine learns of her brother's arrival and was curious to hear how he lived in his short stay at the city. A brother she never met but wished she had the time to catch up with his stories straight from himself.

As they feast upon supper a soldier knocks loudly on the door. Shione walks over to the door,

"Who goes there?" a shaky voice comes through of a man, who was obviously scared,

"Lord Shione, you must hear my words immediately." Shione opens the door and lets the soldier in. the soldier enters and bows to Lady Christa and Lady Catherine,

"I am sorry to disturb you my Ladies but the riders have returned." The soldier looks at Shione and continues to speak,

"A small army of the darkness forces are approaching the city my Lord. The riders say around five hundred men in battle armor and they chant as they march." Shione looks over at Lady Christa puzzled by the news,

"If this is the case why send only five hundred soldiers. They know that our forces have grown by far over the last six months. If they attack us they will surely be slaughtered." The soldier looks down and begins to shiver, looking back up he drops to his knees and begins to choke violently. Shione rushes and holds the man up stopping him from maybe choking to death,

"What's wrong soldier, what aren't you telling us?" The soldier leans over Shione's shoulder and moves his mouth close to his ear,

"Lord Shione, they have seen the devil and the devil possess' through the mind and the body. These aren't any ordinary soldiers my lord. These are devil creatures with the power to float above land." Shione pushes the soldier in front of him to have a clear look at his status. The soldier was pale and his eyes bloodshot. His eyes twitched and he continued to shiver,

"How is this true soldier? There is no such thing as these devil creatures. Are the riders barking mad?" The soldier takes a few large steps backward and smiles, as he smiles blood drips from his gums and his teeth begin to grow in length. The top case of teeth pierces through his lower lip and the soldiers eyes glaze over unclear black,

"If these are not real my Lord then why do I hurt like this? My Lord, if the creatures are not those of the devil then why, why do I have the urge to rip you apart from limb to limb?" Shione steps back and moves between the mutating soldier and Lady Christa and Lady Catherine,

"Pass me my sword my Lady" Lady Christa rises to her feet and throws Shione his sword. She raises her staff and points it toward the soldier. The soldier begins to lift from the floor and hover. Screaming in extreme pain and agony the face of the man morphs, his hair falls out and his face gets stretched back tearing his skin. His ears grow pointed and his body pulses. Pale wings ripped out from his back, spraying blood across the walls. The screaming stops and the beast with his head down looks up,

"Did I forget to mention they can travel from one person to another my Lord?" Lady Catherine raises her magic bow and fires a light blue arrow which strikes the beast in its left wing,

"Summoned from the depths of hell to withstand the strongest of all magic you cannot hurt me." Shione stands ready for battle holding his large sword up high and firm,

"Who has sent you beast?" The creature lowers from hovering in the air and slowly steps one foot down, it kneels and wraps its wings around itself hiding all but its eyes staring at Shione,

Estaban Bridges

"Who else human? but Emperor Glenthoron himself." The beast launches itself at Lord Shione and tackles him to the floor sending him down with a crash. The beast punches at Shione's chest and then raises to his feet and holds Shione up by his head,

"The power we posses is like that of fifty men and we are the dominant species of all that live. We will eventually rule this world and hell will become overwhelmingly destructive. Heaven will collapse at our feet and there will be nobody standing against us." The beast moved toward Lady Christa and looks at the staff she held,

"The only thing which matters is the power compressed within that staff." Suddenly an arrow penetrates through the left wing of the beast; the beast turns to find Lady Catherine standing on guard with her bow and arrow in hand,

"The only thing which matters is survival of us beast." Lady Catherine releases yet another arrow which becomes lodged in the beast's eye socket and impales through his brain. The beast falls to his knees releasing the grasp he had upon Shione who falls to the floor. The beast grasps hold of the arrow and tries persistently to remove it from his skull. Shione meanwhile finds his balance and rises to his feet. Picking his sword up from the floor he holds it to the beast's neck from behind,

"Looks like you're going back from where you came from." With this Shione swings with the up most power and cuts trough the neck of the beast, the beasts head drops to the floor and disintegrates in a small puddle of dust but yet the body of the beast stands and begins to lash out, Lady Christa points her staff at the beast,

Trilogy of Leon

"With the power of time and the wrath of god hold this beast with the strength of ancient vine." Upon completion of the spell the beast was held tightly with mystical force and it was taken to the floor. With a great slam the royal guards rushed into the room with swords drawn. They ran to the beast and began to thrush there swords into the withering body of the beast and after a few fresh wounds the body also disintegrated into a pile of dust and all was quiet. The main royal soldier places his hand upon Shione's shoulder,

"The riders all turned into the same sort of hellish beasts my Lord. We have slain three and just one remains." Shione looks at the two Ladies,

"Are you both ok? Will you be ok here?" Lady Christa and Lady Catherine walk over to each other and some of the royal guards surround them,

"We're fine Shione. Please go and help the others." Shione smiles and bows his head,

"Yes my Lady." Shione proceeds with his soldiers out of the palace leaving Lady Christa and Lady Catherine under protection by the royal guard.

Lady Christa sits with Lady Catherine and they begin to talk,

"That beast, I have never seen any thing of the sort. For us to be able to take on such power we need a more powerful and magical defense force. Especially with so many on the way" Lady Catherine begins to think carefully,

"Mother, what do you suggest?" Lady Christa thinks long and hard,

"Catherine, do you remember Sir Dante and Sir Binor?" Lady Catherine laughs,

"Do I mother? How can I forget? There ever such a pair but they haven't been seen in years. How do you suppose we find them? I agree that they would be a great advantage to our forces but finding them will be near impossible surely." Lady Christa thinks once again very carefully. She stands and walks over to the window and puts her hand out. She whistles a soothing tune and a small bird lands rest upon her hand. The bird was a small robin with an elegant red chest. Lady Christa holds the bird close to her and whispers,

"Little robin. Fly fast and fly high. Find Dante and Binor and tell them Christa beckons there help, for the sake of her life, she needs your help. Fly with great speed little robin and fly safely." As quick as the speed of light the robin disappears from her hand and flies off on its quest to find the strangers.

Meanwhile Shione runs through the streets of the city closely followed by the royal guard soldiers. They follow the screams of pain and eventually come across the beast standing in the middle of the calm stream gardens, the gardens where people of the city sat in silence and had chance to think over things clearly, a place to relax now turned into a bloody field full of dead bodies and showered in blood. The beast defended itself as three soldiers poked at it with pikes. One by one each soldier had his head ripped off and then there dead bodies dropped to the floor as blood came gushing out. Shione stood there backed with ten soldiers all with weapons drawn. Slowly they coarsely moved toward the beast. The beast turns and faces them, blood dripping from his mouth and wounds covering his body. The beasts were greater in size than the humans they had took as there hosts. The beast they were facing was as tall as two large men. Its wings span was twenty metres from tip to tip. It growls deeply at the oncoming soldiers,

"You can't kill me humans. You will all die like the others laying around me" Shione stands clutching his sword,

"We can't just let you be beast. How many more have to suffer if we turn our backs. Id rather I die than anybody else." The beast roars and points at Shione,

"Then die you will foolish human." The beast runs toward Shione and his men, it picks up two of the soldiers as it approaches Shione. With two soldiers still in its grasp the beast jumps high and pounds on another soldier crushing his body as easily as if it were just a leaf. Shione drives his sword through one of the beast's legs just as he runs between them. The beast kicks back hitting Shione and sending him to his knees. While quickly turning around the beast smashes the heads together of the two soldiers he had in his hands and drops them to the floor. Shione raises his hand,

"Wind twist and turn make this beast churn." The beast is instantly thrown into the air and slammed into the ground at a breathtaking speed. Being lifted back into the air the beast revolves in circles while constantly being flipped around. As this is happening the beast flaps its wings trying to regain control of itself but it proves useless. Shione lowers his hand and the beast is hammered onto the floor so hard that it makes the ground unearth and ripple all around the landing zone. Straight away the soldiers run over and begin to brutally attack the beast in his weakened state. Shione joins his soldiers and walks over to the beast. Standing by its head he lifts his sword,

"You didn't kill me beast." Shione stamps his sword through the forehead of the beast cracking through its skull. The beast groans as its life is drained away and the body releases all tension. Like the others killed before, it then cracked up and turned into dust which started being blown away in the wind. Shione stands back and looks around. He looks at the situation and is confronted by the image of headless bodies. Bodies ripped in two. Blood dripping off trees, the sign of a brutal and bloody battle. The soldiers that were left stood behind Shione. He looks down while replacing his sword back in the holster,

"Maybe we will have a much harder battle than I originally thought." He turns to the soldiers,

"I know that it's horrible my fellow swordsman but please these soldiers must be given a proper burial and the same goes for the city folk who have lost there lives this evening." The soldiers all nod in acceptance of there orders and Shione returns on his way to the palace.

Back at the palace Lady Christa and Lady Catherine wait patiently for Shione's return. Catherine turns to her mother,

"So, if Leon was born two years before me mother I guess he never knew about me?" Lady Christa looked away,

"I never mentioned you to Leon because he had much to learn about the past. If he had been with us longer I would have let him know and I'm sure he would have been desperate to meet you" Lady Catherine walks over to the window looking out at the moon slightly covered by the clouds,

Trilogy of Leon

"When will the ceremony take place mother?" Lady Christa also stands and walks over to the window and puts her arm around Catherine,

"I see your looking at the statue in his honour. The ceremony will take place tomorrow at midday and then you will get to meet him." Lady Catherine sighs depressingly,

"Its going to be strange mother, the statue is how he looked but when and if we bring him back he will look nothing like he once did. Is it really my brother, your son were bringing back or is it just a copy, something unreal?" Lady Christa smiles happily,

"It is the soul that makes a person not the body. A soul could be in any body and it would not change the slightest bit. The body we will raise will be that of Leon's my child. Although he will not look the same he will be the same inside." Catherine turns to Lady Christa and steps away from the window,

"I will get some rest mother for tomorrow will be a long day. Is my chamber still where it used to be?"

"It is indeed. Just because you went on travels to find yourself doesn't mean I would have thrown you out of your old room. I know how much you like the space." Lady Catherine opens the door,

"Love you mother." She walks out followed by two of the royal guard and the door is closed behind them. Lady Christa turns once again and looks outside of the window,

"I love you to child. You will not be going into battle, I cannot face losing another." Lady Christa shreds a tear of sorrow which runs down her face and drips silently to the floor. A quiet knock comes from the door and Shione enters,

"My lady, all of the beasts have been slain. Maybe you should get some rest." Lady Christa looks over at Shione and smiles looking strangely into his eyes. Shione looks slightly away and looks back at Lady Christa,

"You ok my Lady, have I got a cut on my face?" Shione starts feeling across his face to see if he had sustained a wound in battle and Lady Christa giggles,

"No Shione. I was just thinking that's all." Shione walks closer toward her,

"Anything you'd like to talk about my Lady?" She runs her hand smoothly through her hair moving it slightly over her face,

"Shione I was thinking. You're always here to protect me. You are always here to confide in. You've done a lot for me and I'd like to take this moment to say thank you, thank you." Shione shakes his head,

"No my Lady, there is no need to do such a thing at all." She moves closer to Shione and places her hands around his waist,

"Shione, please just call me Christa." She wraps her arms around him and pulls him close. Tightly she hugs him and so Shione puts his arms around her also. She moves away and kisses him softly upon the cheek,

"Goodnight Shione, sleep well." She leaves the room leaving Shione standing where he was. Left him red faced and thinking deeply about the situation just passed.

Early morning and all was bright. The birds sang there songs from the roof tops and from the trees as the city folk did there daily chores. Lord Shione awakes and steps out of his bed to find Lady Catherine sitting in the corner of the room,

"Oh, I'm sorry my lady have I woke up late?" Lady Catherine raises from her seat and steps toward the door,

"No Shione you haven't, I just wanted to wait for you to wake so I could say to you that we have quite a wild day ahead of us and that" She pauses for a second,

"That I want you to stay close to mother for she is very vulnerable at this time and also. She does like you a lot incase you haven't already realized" Shione smiles and looks down at his feet,

"As you wish my Lady. I shall stay close to Lady Christa and I shall be at her service for the full day" Lady Catherine opens the door slightly and peers out,

"Thank you Shione oh and maybe you should have a well earned wash before you come to meet us. Mother would very much like that." With a cheeky smirk Catherine leaves the room closing the door quietly behind her. Shione sits down on his bed and holds his head in his hands. He looks back up thinking deeply to himself and walks over to the mirror on the wall,

"I'm not that dirty surely." Shione continues to get dressed thinking what he should do regarding Lady Christa.

A group of ten royal guard soldiers walk through the palace hallways and enter the room of light. A room dedicated to god and light, hope and love. They stand in front of the doors and withdraw there swords holding them down at there sides. To the left of an alter Lady Christa stood, while Lady Catherine stood to the right.

A bowl sat upon the Alter and around it a few different items. Catherine looks into Lady Christa's eyes,

"Why are you scared mother?" Lady Christa looks at the soldiers standing guard,

"I fear that we might fail my child" Catherine lifts Christa's hand and holds it softly,

"If we fail then there's always tomorrow so be strong mother." Lady Christa holds Catherine's other hand,

"Shall we start?" Catherine smiles and nods her head slightly. Christa picks up a small amount of purple leafs from beside the bowl and takes a breath to talk when suddenly Shione rushes through the doors to the room. His hair was tied back and his face was washed immaculate. All his cloths were fresh and he walked over to the alter,

"I'm sorry I'm late my Lady" Christa smiles and looks at Shione from up to down and back up again looking at his eyes,

"That's ok Shione, you look very presentable today. Anybody would think you were dressing up for Leon" Shione frowns,

"Not at all my Lady it's just that." He looks at Lady Catherine who was stood grinning and looking with a mischief sort of expression,

"Doesn't matter my Lady, please continue." Lady Christa turns her head back to the Alter and Shione steps behind her. Christa proceeds and drops the leafs into the bowl,

"With the life within these mystic leafs may the life of the earth be collected." Lady Catherine pours some water into the bowl which was mixed with natural stone as she said,

Trilogy of Leon

"With the source of this holy water may the generation of flesh be made?" The two of them cup the remaining ingredients in there hands and place them in the mixture. Both of them chanting quietly,

"With the power of the alpha and the omega the strength of the gods may Leon restore with holy life. May he be resurrected to return for the good of the light and to redeem all of darkness. May the gods save his soul?" Lady Christa and Catherine stand silent for a few moments. Neither a whisper nor a breeze shattered any lack of movement or silence. They waited and waited but still nothing happened. No sign. All those within the room thought about the possibility of failure and what consequence this will have upon future events. Shione walks behind Lady Christa and places his hand firmly on her shoulder,

"There's always tomorrow my Lady." She turned and looked in his eyes and raised her hand to hold his,

"But is there Shione?" Looking to the floor she turns and makes for the exit. The soldiers guarding the doors move out of her way and she leaves the room with the guards following. Shione looks over and smiles slightly at Lady Catherine,

"How do you feel?" Catherine walks away from the Alter and stops. Standing in the doorway, without looking back, she emotionally speaks,

"My mother is giving up hope Shione. I can see it in her eyes and I can sense it from when we speak. She feels the city will be lost but she is ready to sacrifice her life before it does. Is there really any hope left?" she continues to walk out of the room to pursue Lady Christa. Shione stands in deep thought. The world closes around him and

Estaban Bridges

he thinks of as many possibilities that he could but all that clouded his mind was the fact that if Lady Christa gave her life for the good of the people and for the sake of a strand of hope then what would be left. Who would he be left with? The answers to these questions he had to find.

Late afternoon Shione sat in the calm stream gardens. Lady Catherine and Christa remained in the palace. The light had begun to dim and the city folk began to go to there homes in time for dinner. The city was fairly silent and you could hear the birds clearly at the tops of trees. Shockingly a loud high pitched howl breaches the city walls followed by a sudden silence. Shione jumps to his feet and instantly runs toward the city gates. On the way he stumbles across a soldier. The soldier grabs him. Speaking shaken the soldier asks,

"My Lord what was that sound? Is it the devil creatures?" Shione shakes him slightly holding onto his shoulders,

"Lad, run to the palace. Tell them I order the city bell to be rung. All soldiers to there stations and be certain that all of the royal guard are protecting the Lady Christa and Lady Catherine in the palace. Understand?" The soldier withdraws his sword,

"Yes sir. Right away." Straight away the soldier runs to the palace while Shione reaches the city gates. Already at the gates were a large handful of the city soldiers ready and waiting for orders. Shione stops running and walks over to the soldiers who instantly without orders move into lined formation. One of the generals steps forward,

"Sir. We have known about this attack since yesterday sir so we have kept prepared. Were here to fight for freedom sir and were all willing to do what is in doubtfully necessary." Shione grasps hold of the generals hand and shakes it with the up most respect,

"Thank you soldier." Shione speaks louder,

"Thank all of you brave souls. We have a hard battle on our hands. May the light and god himself be on our sides this afternoon and lets walk away from this with our heads held high, do you hear me?" Like an unbreakable team of superior soldiers un-afraid of death they lift there weapons up to the sky. In one large grouped reply they shout confidently,

"For hope and life sir." Shione begins to relay his tactical plan to the general pointing at where he wanted soldiers stationed in an attempt to defend against intrusion incase the city gates failed to hold against the invasion. Shione continues,

"Also general give me ten of those men. Your best archers, put the on the ledges overlooking the walls." The general turns to the men and starts deploying the teams and Shione runs up the steps leading to the ledges looking out over the moat. Hiding behind one of the raised parts of the city wall he moved his head around so he was able to look down toward the empty land between the city and the moat. What he saw was the most disturbing of all he must have ever seen. Five hundred or more men screamed and rolled across the ground. Some of them tearing off there cloths and body armour. The ground could be seen stained in blood as wings of hell sprung through the men's backs ripping apart there skin which remained hanging off there body's. As Shione continued to watch the strange bloody evolution of the men groups of the hell like creatures emerged. Eventually not one of the human hosts was left standing. Stood in an unformatted formation was now five hundred or so fully mutated hell beasts like those which were slain within the city walls the day before. Shione stopped looking and leans his back against the wall. He dropped his head back and looks up at the sky. He looks at the stars slowly beginning to appear and wonders into his own imagination. He begins to imagine how it would be if the attack by the darkness was successful. He thinks about the entire city being wiped out, all the woman and children who would be murdered and the creatures not having a care in the world but simply enjoying the deaths of others. He gets around to thinking of his own death and how it might be. He thinks to himself that no matter how he died that in the end it wouldn't really matter because no matter how he tries and how far he will get he will be sure to fail. His hope dies to a mere drop and his heart sinks. Quickly his mind jumps to Lady Christa and the death that she would sustain. A tear emerges from his eyes all travels down the side of his face. Furthermore the darkness getting the most powerful weapon on the face of the earth would throw the world into suffocation and all that is good would be choked to death and disappear. This is something he had to fight to stop. He had to fight to defend the earth and to protect the heavens but again he thinks back to what if it fails. What if it isn't good enough? All the struggle and determination would be a waste of time which could be so precious to be spent on other things like love and happiness. The though of this makes another tear drift and slowly drip down his face and hit the floor. A voice comes from as if afar but yet so close,

"Shione my friend, you are stronger than this. Don't give up on yourself. Don't give up on the people." Shione awakes from deep thought to see a man standing before him. Slowly looking from the legs of the man, he drifts his eyes upward to find a topless large built man standing with his arms crossed. The man looked down at him grinning. He offers his hand as a boost for Shione to rise to his feet. Shione has a closer look at the man who had bright blue eyes but there was something different. The centers of his eyes instead of being black were pure white. His hair was long and straight. His face muscular like the rest of his built. The man smiles,

"What's wrong Shione, you don't recognize an old friend?" Shione takes a moment and realized,

"Leon, Leon is it you?" The man puts out his hand once more and shakes the hand of Shione holding with a tight respectful grip,

"It is me Shione. I feel like never before. I feel I have the strength of many men and I just feel." He puts out his arms and opens his hands,

"I feel like a god." Shione smile with the hope he had lost being flushed back into his heart and soul,

"I am so glad to see you Leon my lad but this is no time for celebration. Have you seen the situation we are in?" Leon walks and stands in full view between two of the raised parts of the wall and has a good look at the beasts scrambling around. He turns to Shione,

"What are these creatures like?" Shione shakes his head in gesture that the answer is not positive,

"Just one can take out a large group of men Leon. They have so much strength that I have never seen anything like it before. They can hover above land itself. With that many, I really don't think we will stand a very good chance at all." Leon laughs loudly,

"These beasts are nothing more than goats we receive our milk from Shione how on earth." Stopped in mid conversation Leon and Shione are confronted by one of the beasts which lands on top of the city walls right beside them. The beast growls and stretches while its wings expand fully intimidating Leon and Shione. They quickly run for cover behind a few barrels not to far away from where they had been standing. Leon whispers over to Shione,

"You said they hovered. You didn't say they could actually fly." Shione shrugs his shoulders,

"I didn't know honestly." They hear the beast stepping loudly over to the barrels and they look up to see the beast standing over them looking around and sniffing moving its nose higher in the air. Leon points to the barrels and puts his hands out questioning Shione what was inside of them. Shione shrugs his shoulders once again. Looking back at the beast they watch as a few arrows propel through the air and strike the beast. A couple hit its wing and a couple hit its chest. It turns from the barrels and jumps down to the forecourt behind the city gates from where the arrows had been shot and begins to attack the armed guards. Leon and Shione quickly stand and look down seeing the beast being bombarded with arrows and impaled with spikes and swords. The beast bursts into a shower of dust and all is quiet. The soldiers regroup awaiting the next attack. Shione looks at Leon,

"We will be able to get you a sword from down the forecourt and then we just need to wait." The two of them run down the steps and Leon arms himself with the sharpest sword he could find. As Leon and Shione run to the front of the formation of soldiers the city gates begin to be knocked. The gates vibrate as the beast's launch themselves at them trying to break through. A crack appears along one of the gates and with each pound of the door the crack becomes larger. A majority of the city army arrives in aid fully equipped and ready for battle and line up behind the other soldiers. The soldier who Shione gave the orders to at the beginning of the situation runs up to him,

"Lord Shione. We have many men still getting equipped sir and they will shortly be here. The royal guards have barricaded themselves within the palace and we have men at the foot of the palace steps." Shione pats the soldier on the shoulder,

"Good man. Get prepared for battle soldier." As the man runs into formation the gates get broken into two and the beasts pile on top of each other pushing to get through the small gap. As the pushing and shoving persists the door widens and the archers shoot there arrows at the beasts which could be seen. Constantly they rain there arrows down on the creatures but it does little good. Finally the gates give way and crash to the floor. The creature's closest to the gates fall to the floor as the gates give way and the creatures behind them pile over into the forecourt. Leon and Shione charge over to the offensive attack and defend with almighty swings of there swords. Slicing through the rough skin of the creatures they run constantly in order to not be knocked to there feet. The soldiers charge forward and crowd in around the beasts slicing at there legs at up into there body's. The creatures retaliated by stamping on the soldiers and crushing them to the floor. They pick up and throw random soldiers a far distance knocking them unconscious on the floor or against the walls. They bite ravenously and decapitate soldiers making blood spray high in the air. Soldiers lives are took at a wink of an eye. Lives lost to a desperate fight for survivor. It wasn't about hope anymore. It was about keeping yourself alive. Leon with his new found power hits strike after strike onto creature after creature. His sword snaps into as if it were nothing more than a thin piece of wood and so he raises the beasts of there feet and throws them to the floor. He picks them up and knocks down a group of the beasts by running and using the beast as a battering ram. Off a dead body of his fellow soldier he picks up a dagger and jumps onto the knee of one of the beasts and jumps onto the back of another stabbing and cutting, sawing and twisting until the beasts head is detached and blown into dust. Shione turns and turns looking all around him to see clouds of dust drifting toward the floor and bodies lying all across the ground. Some men continued to breathe and shout for help. Some shout help me, help me god while others cry and hold there hands to there eyes. A few of them take the experience as to much and feel they will never survive. Out of pure feel they take there daggers and drive them through there chests. Ending there own lives seems the only way out. None of them could even imagine the toughness of the battle at hand. None of them could imagine the carnage they would see. Shione realizes the battle at the forecourt has already been lost and so orders the retreat to the bottom of the palace gates. Anybody who could walk or run retreated toward the palace with Shione following last, he looks back to see Leon still standing at the forecourt battling his way through a few of the hell monsters at a time. He shouted,

Trilogy of Leon

"This way Leon, we shall regroup at the palace." Leon looks over and began to run toward Shione but his route got cut off when one of the creatures landed foot in front of him. As Leon battled his way to get through he shouts to Shione,

"Go ahead my friend I shall do what I can here. Just protect my mother." Shione takes the instruction and continues on his path to the palace.

As the battle at the foot of the palace takes place Leon is left alone fighting at the front gates in the forecourt. All of the beasts had now entered the city so the doorway to the city remained open and clear. Leon continued to battle five of the monsters when he struck one in the chest and then sliced upwards cutting the beast in two. As the beast disappeared so did the other four. Blasts of fire had been shot and had burnt the beasts without a second delay. Leon turned and looked at the direction of where the blasts had come from. At the front gate were two strange looking men on the backs of two small dragons. A small robin flies over and lands on Leon's shoulder. Happily chirping it then flew off toward the palace. One man on the left was of medium sized build. He had long dark fair hair and wore a long leather jacket. He had black boots and a black waistcoat with a silver belt also he wore tight leather gloves with spikes sticking out along the knuckles. Along the one side of his face he had a tribal tattoo which went down along his neck. On his back he had a large sword and he had small throwing knives in a special holster going diagonally across his chest. The man on the right was fairly large built. His arms were so large that he wore a sleeveless brown jacket. Across the length of his arms he had tattoos of dragons and daggers. He wore brown torn trousers and had short hair, as if almost bold. He held a staff about four feet long, on the top of the staff it had a small figure of a dragon molded from pure gold. At the same time both of the men stepped off the dragons and started walking toward Leon. Not knowing the strangers at hand Leon raises his sword and points it at them,

"Stay where you are." The two men stop and look at each other and then look back at Leon. The small one laughs and mentions,

"My friend, if we wanted to fight and kill you." The larger man continues the speech,

"We would have of done it already." Then the small man speaks again,

"We have been asked to come to the beautiful City of Savon." Again the larger man speaks,

"Because her Lady Christa asked for our help and we have known her for years now and for years to come. So here to help." Once again the smaller man speaks,

"Is myself, Sir Dante and my good friend here, Sir Binor? Here at the Lady's service. It's a pleasure to meet you?" They wait for a reply. Leon lowers his sword,

"Leon. I am Lady Christa's son. I thank you for your help back then." Dante looks at Binor,

"Well I never would have guessed this man here is the Lady's son. Well not a second to lose, where are the rest of the little creatures?" Leon jumps to attention and begins to run to the palace waving for Dante and Binor to follow,

"This way my friends, the palace is under attack as we speak." The three of them run through the city at great

Trilogy of Leon

speed eagerly wanting more violence and to battle to there heart content.

Meanwhile the retreat to the foot of the palace gates had fully been completed and the battle was still under way. The majority of the beasts had followed the soldiers to the destination but a few had gone different places within the city causing havoc and demolishing through houses. Ripping places apart, as if they were nothing more than thin pieces of paper. Leon and the two new companions reach the intense battle scene. They stand and check over the situation. Realizing there didn't seem to be many of the creatures left Leon turns to Dante and Binor,

"There's something wrong here my friends. Only a few have gone elsewhere in the city and apart from the ones before us, where are the others?" all of them glance up at the palace but see nothing incriminating as to say forced entry from anywhere over the building. Binor suddenly steps forward pointing up toward the top of the palace,

"Look!" They all follow his sight to see the beasts had flown up to the top of the palace and were trying to get in through a small balcony, which lead to steps leading into the centre of the palace itself. Dante reaches for a small whistle connected to a chain around his neck. He whistles through it releasing a heavenly sound. Binor stepped further forward still looking up to the balcony. He lifted his staff which he had been holding since first encounter at the city gates. He mutters in his deep voice,

"The winged demon chained to the seal of god. Fly high and fly strong. These creatures are in the wrong; expel them from the land they have trod." The small gold molded dragon statue on the top of the staff lit a bright red. The statue began to increase in size and a small bird like creature was left holding on with its claws to the top of the staff. The creature which was totally red stretched out its wings and let out a loud growl. Binor lifted the staff and so the creature leaped off flapping its wings. The creature started to fly up toward the balcony but magnificently as it flew it became larger in size. It stopped growing and was left a giant size. Its wings span around fifty metre across and its body was huge. Truly it was a dragon of all the dragons. A magical chain slightly invisible to the human eye, connected from the dragons leg to the other end of the chain which connected against the staff which Binor was holding onto with all his might. Leon looks in amazement and Dante shakes his shoulder,

"D'ya see that my friend. That there is Binor's here little pet. It's actually a demon creature which we caught. Its great isn't it? Watch what's next." Dante looks back up toward the dragon rubbing his hands together and smiling. He chuckled a laugh and whispered over to Binor,

"Do it brother. Do it." Binor pulls the staff slightly and the dragon flew up close right next to the balcony. The beast pushing to get into the steps stop and they all look around to see this huge beast staring at the. Especially that the dragon was at least twice the size of them. Two of the beasts look at each other and then run toward the edge of the balcony. Stepping onto the barrier around the edge of the balcony they fire themselves at the dragon and cling onto it with the long claws. Wildly biting and scratching at the dragon, the dragon tries to get them off by shaking but they continued to hold themselves on. The dragon stops and hovers in midair. It puts out its wings fully and bends its back backward. It takes a slow long big breath as the beasts continue to attack it. As the dragon continues to take its breath another one of the hell creatures jumps off the balcony and digs its claws into the chest of the dragon but still the dragon did not move or even shiver. The dragon's eyes turn fiercely the color of burning wood and it lets out a shriek of what seemed like pain. It was so loud and so ear piercing all the soldiers on the floor had to cover there ears and the hell creatures stumbled in agony as the screech went through them. The whole battle seemed to cease to take place as the shriek was taking place. Anybody who was able to looked up to see what was making such a noise and saw the dragon. The dragon shred a tear of blood from its eye as its body begun to heat up. In a second the body of the dragon engulfed into flames sending the hell beasts to there graves as instantly they got cremated with the heat. The dragon looks toward the balcony and flew closer toward the doorway. Still being able to see beasts inside trying to push there way down the tight staircase he makes and endless river of flame from within him and sends it shooting down making any creature in contact burst into dust. The hell beasts left down on the ground remain shocked and stunned by the screeching which had gone through them. Blood had emerged from inside of there heads and other heads of the beasts had exploded under the pressure. The two dragons which had been left at the front gate walked up behind Leon, Dante and Binor. The one rubbed the bottom of its chin on the top of Dante and purred calmly. Dante places his hand on the dragons nose and rubs it gently,

"Hello beautiful." The other dragon walks over to Binor and places its head down on the floor pushing between his legs. Binor raises his hand,

"Return Pofacsus." The dragon up by the balcony extinguishes and returns itself quickly. Reversing the process it reduces in size as it flew back toward the staff. It landed on top of the staff, holding on with its claws and disappeared. The small dragon statue ceased to shine any longer. Binor's dragon gave a little nudge and walked forward. Binor got picked up by the dragons head and slid down its neck landing smoothly and softly in the seat on the dragons back. Dante and Binor both nodded at each other and Dante jumped onto the back of his dragon. Leon looked up at the two superior dragon trainers,

"The whistle, is it your communication with the beasts?" Dante smiled,

"Not beasts, my friend but our companions. They are our family." Dante and Binor take off toward the remaining beasts as Leon runs toward the way they were heading. The soldiers at the foot of the palace return to formation but Shione was nowhere to be seen. The remaining creatures are slain by Dante and Binor as they flew above them. Dante flew and landed in front of one of the beasts. His dragon opened fire and shot a large raging fire ball which demolished through the creature leaving it to burst into dust. Binor flew straight into the final beast and his dragon sank its claws into the beast picking it off the ground. As they rose into the air the dragon detached the head of the beast by ripping it off with its sharp teeth and again this beast burst into a shower of dust which floated away in the wind. All was now quiet. Soldiers on the ground saw to the wounded and began to move out around the city to help anybody in need. Dante and Binor rejoined Leon on the ground and they sent the dragons to guard the front of the city, at the city gates, due to the gates being destroyed. Leon looks around still not being able to see Shione in sight. He grasps hold of one soldier running past,

"Soldier, where is Lord Shione? Have you seen him?" The soldier shook his head and replied,

"No sir. Last I saw of Lord Shione he was fighting one of the hell creatures and after that I did not see him." The soldier continued on his way and Leon turned toward Dante and Binor,

"I thank you for your help. From what I have seen your brave men." The two of them relaxed, standing without saying a word. Leon continued to think about what could have happened to Shione. The palace gates opened and a small force of the royal Guards walked out. They walked and lined each side of the palace steps. When all were in position Lady Christa and Lady Catherine proceeded to walk out and down the steps. Leon, Dante and Binor walked quickly to the bottom of the steps to meet them. When Lady Christa and Catherine saw them they smiled happily and ran down the steps giving them both hugs,

"How glad I am to see you both. Thank you for both coming. I knew you would." Lady Christa smiles at them both. They bow there heads,

"As soon as we got the message off the little bird my lady we came at great speed. Anything for you and Lady Catherine." All was quiet as they bathed in the reunion. Lady Christa glanced over at Leon standing behind Dante and Binor. Not realizing who he was due to his new body she asks Dante,

Estaban Bridges

"Who is your new friend Dante?" He looks puzzled and confused at Leon and looks back at Lady Christa,

"I'm sorry ma'am but I do not understand." Leon steps forward and stands in front of Dante and Binor. He holds Lady Christa's hand. Binor scratches his head also confused. Leon closes his eyes and bows his head down. Looking back up his eyes glaze over with tears,

"It's me, Leon mother." Lady Christa quite rightfully shocked pulls away from Leon and looks into his eyes,

"Is it really you my son? We thought the spell was a failure." Lady Catherine moves closer to have a closer look at her brother. Leon holds Christa's hand once again,

"It is me mother and I can assure you the spell was highly successful. You have successfully revived me from my death and I return much stronger in this new body." Lady Christa puts her arm around Catherine and pulls her closer,

"Leon I would like you to meet your sister, Catherine. She's been waiting to meet you and we have spoken a lot about you." With it being Leon's turn for a surprise he is also took back and becomes astonished with the news,

"Sister, well it's nice to meet you. I'm sure we will have much time to talk and share our stories." Lady Catherine nods in excitement,

"Yes, yes indeed brother" The companionship of the five close family and friends stand all staring at each other, the feeling of love and care being released. Lady Christa looks around awakening from the little atmosphere between them all,

"May I ask where Shione is?" Not knowing the answer they all look around and at each other expecting each

Trilogy of Leon

other to know the answer to the very important question. Leon is the first to answer,

"He hasn't been seen since he was battling against one of the beasts. Since then he hasn't appeared or been found." Lady Christa begins to worry deeply in her heart that Shione may have been killed when a soldier runs over. He was wounded in the arm with a deep gash. His cloths were blood stained and his face grazed. He steps between the five of them,

"My Lady, I have news about Lord Shione which I think you should hear." Lady Christa becomes very interested in the soldiers news,

"Please, tell me." The soldier coughs and holds his arm,

"Lord Shione. I saw him being lifted by one of those things and the beast flew away holding him as a couple of the other beasts followed close behind." Lady Christa holds the man by his shoulders increasingly worried,

"Which way were they heading?" The soldier removes himself from the grip of Lady Christa and takes a step backward,

"They headed towards the front gates my Lady but that was the last thing I saw before I was injured myself." The man bowed and ran off again quickly through the crowd of injured soldiers and helping city folk. Lady Christa turns to Leon. Leon looks into her eyes,

"I don't understand how they would have got past us because we ran straight from the front gates mother." Dante stepped forward,

"They could have flown over the city walls as we were on our way here." Lady Christa looks at the three men standing in line,

"Leon. Dante and Binor. Please give chase and hunt them down. I want Shione back alive and I want him back as soon as possible. We can't afford to lose him." Lady Catherine also steps to the side of the three men,

"Mother I shall go to. I could help with my magic and it would give them the extra advantage." Lady Christa shakes her head,

"You shall do no such thing. You will stay with me in the palace." Lady Catherine looks down depressed and steps back beside Lady Christa. Dante steps backward a few steps,

"Let's go get Shione." Binor follows Dante's lead but Leon looks between the to of them,

"You both have dragons how am I supposed to keep up with that speed?" he looks at his mother,

"Where is Savior?" Lady Christa looks at one of the royal guards,

"Please go and get Savior, hurry." The soldier runs hastily away and Leon looks at Dante and Binor,

"I shall meet you at the front gate shortly." With this they walk away toward the gates. Leon mentions to Lady Christa,

"The front gates were destroyed in the attack and so we our vulnerable. I suggest you send constant guard and get the gates reinstated as soon as possible mother." Lady Catherine bows her head at Leon,

"Take care brother and may god be with you on your journey. Please excuse me." She turns and begins her way up the steps back toward the palace. The soldier returns upon Savior and steps down passing Leon the reigns. Leon runs his hand through Saviors mane and down his face,

"I'm back brother." Leon jumps up onto his back and looks down at Lady Christa,

"We will bring him back. I promise." He turns and gallops toward the front gates to meet Dante and Binor. Lady Christa thinks deeply to herself hoping that they do return with Shione. She also retreats back to the palace where she is once again placed under royal guard.

Leon rides without stopping through where the gates once stood. He runs past Dante on the one side of the entrance and Binor on the other side of the entrance. They begin to move and pick up pace. They both jump off the ground and fly closely either side behind Leon galloping at great speed. Within a minute or two they cross the moat and continue on there way to find the beasts that had stolen Shione.

After a few hours of riding they came across one of the beasts lying on the ground. The beast seemed as if it had no energy and it seemed drained of life. In the darkness they sat and watched as it rolled over and tried to pick itself up off the floor. Its wings draped over its back and lay along the floor. Dante looks over and questions Leon,

"What do you think is wrong with it? Shall we kill it?" Leon steps off Savior and brings his sword out defending himself as he walked close toward it. The beast saw that Leon was approaching and growled quietly while trying to claw through the ground in an attempt to crawl away. As Leon got closer he saw that the creature was severely wounded and one thing stuck out in particular. The beast had a dagger through its one eye. Blood almost black was still dripping out, Leon looked up,

"The dagger through the beast eye is slowly draining it of its blood. This beast will bleed to death." Binor gets his dragon to poke its tail at the beast to see if it had any sudden reaction but the beast did not react. Binor speaks deeply,

"This beast is truly on deaths door once more where I believed it came from anyway. Is the dagger in its eye that of Lord Shione Leon?" kneeling down in front of the beast Leon yanks the dagger from its eye. It squeals quietly and then it lays its head on the floor. Instead of it bursting into dust it remained alive and seemed depressingly inactive. Binor steps down from his dragon and walks over beside Leon in front of the beast. Binor puts his hand on top of the beasts head and asks Leon,

"Will you put the beast out of its misery Leon?" Leon rises to his feet and steps away from the creature,

"No I will not. The dagger is that of Shione's so he may well be alive." He puts the dagger in support of his belt and climbs back onto Savior. Binor looks over at Dante,

"What do you think my friend?" Dante looks away and looks back,

"It could prove useful to do so." Leon looks between them,

"What is it you are thinking of doing Binor?" without answering Binor puts his staff onto the beasts head. He mutters,

"The beast which is laid before me, lock him into chains and return its soul. Heal this beast and let it no longer flee. Bring this beast to the power of me." The dragon statue on the top of the staff lights up an intense bright white light. The darkness of the night lightens

Trilogy of Leon

all around them and the light engulfs around the beast. When the light withdraws the beast had disappeared. The statue of the dragon returned to normal and Binor walked calmly back to his Dragon and sat back upon it. Leon looks over at him,

"What did you just do to the beast Binor?" Binor smiled proud of himself and sat up straight,

"I have taken him under my wing and now he has a soul he serves me. His power is now part of my power. Also we have a new companion to show us the way to where Lord Shione is." Leon impressed by the power of Binor smirks and nods his head,

"That's very impressive Binor." Straight away Binor lifts the staff and mutters,

"The new creature given a soul, saved from being dammed to hell. Show us to our friend and gain yourself a worthy shell." As before the small golden dragon statue lights up and the beast appears upon the top of the staff. It jumps off onto the ground and stretches its wings and kneels onto the floor with its wings wrapped around itself. The beast had been fully restored and didn't have a scratch or graze on its body. As with the large dragon earlier at the city, the hellish creature had a magical chain. It was connected from its foot to the staff, thus stopping it from escaping if it wanted to. Leon looks in amazement still impressed by the power which he had been shown,

"Binor, how do you mean about the shell?" Binor replied,

"If he were to help us then he will gain a shell of protection. Meaning as with my other family, the other creatures I have captured. They will remain good and well instead of being left to rot in the depths of hell. All

I ask is for the help in battle and other times when it is needed." Leon looks back at the creature still hiding within its wings,

"I suppose you can say that is fair enough." The beast, now companion stands up and hovers above the ground. It growls down at the three men,

"Follow me they are not far." The beast begins to pull to move and so sure enough Binor begins to follow the lead on top of his dragon with Dante and Leon following behind.

Meanwhile back at the City of Savon the repair to the city gates had been underway. The battle field at the courtyard and at the foot of the palace had been cleaned. Any lost bodies were gathered at the city cathedral and they had been buried with all of there names in great honour. Lady Christa and Catherine were waiting patiently in the palace for the return of Leon and the others. Orders had been given to make the city gates thicker and harder to cause more of a defense toward future attacks upon the city. Metal bars as thick as logs were being molded as barriers behind the gates to hold them firm against any battering ram which could be used and large spike were being formed extra sharp to mold onto the front of the gates so that any creature or persons pushing against it would be impaled. A hundred soldiers stood watch over the gates constantly against any possible approaching enemies. From the distance a figure was noticed upon a large horse. The general of the guard squad looked from above the gates on the city walls. He stood between two of the raised parts of the wall staring at the figure. A soldier next to the general questions,

Trilogy of Leon

"Sir, can you see him clearly? Do you believe he may be a threat?" The general sighed,

"If this man was indeed a threat then why would he be stood still upon his horse waving a white flag?" The soldier squints' his eyes to try to see the man clearer,

"It could be a trick Sir. To try and get us to go out." The general turned and began to walk down the steps,

"I don't believe so my friend. I have a good feeling about this. He bears the armor of the Shangerians." The general jumps onto his horse and clicks his fingers at a few of the soldiers. They begin to follow on foot as the general left the front gates and trotted slowly and curiously toward the moat. They got to the moat and the soldiers who had followed on foot raised the bow and arrows all of them aiming on the stranger. Without lowering the moat bridge the general shouts over at the man,

"What brings you here traveler? What business do you have with the people of the City of Savon?" The man from across the moat lowers the white flag and removes his helmet reveling his face,

"I bring a message from King Shudae of the Shangerian people sir. It is a message that the Lady Christa must see at once for it is of great importance." The general thinks hard whether to trust the soldier or whether to send him on his way without letting him come any further. The general questions,

"How can I believe you and trust that this is your true intention messenger?" The man over the moat dismounts from his horse. He begins to shout back over,

"Just two days ago sir, the Kings only son and my queen were slaughtered in cold blood by the darkness. We have done nothing but serve for the darkness in an attempt to keep our people out of harms way but we were proven wrong." The general shrugs his shoulders,

"And how does this affect the people of this city?" the soldier continues,

"We no longer wish to be slaves in our own land sir. We wish to be free and able to live life once again. This is what my message concerns for the Lady Christa." The general again thinks hard about the situation and what could and could not be at stake. He signals for the soldiers to lower there arms and they do so almost unwillingly,

"Lower the bridge." the general orders. As soon as said the bridge begins to lower. It halts as it hits the ground on the other side and the soldier begins to walk over the bridge bringing his horse with him.

Back at the palace the general and only five soldiers escort the visitor through the palace hallways and they reach the throne room. The general steps in front of the visitor and puts his arm out to stop him going any further,

"I must ask for your sword and any other weapon you may have soldier for the safety of the Lady." Instantly the messenger hands over his sword and a small dagger which was attached to his belt. The general checks him over for any concealed weapons and failing to find any he knocks loudly on the throne room door. The door is opened by royal guard from within the throne room and they enter. Kneeling in front of Lady Christa and Catherine the general explains the situation,

"My Lady, before you I bring a messenger. He is from the City of Shangedain. He was sent by King Shudae himself." Lady Christa stands and steps down from the thrown. She walks calmly and slowly over to the general

Trilogy of Leon

and places her hand on his head. He raises to his feet and stands slightly in front but next to the messenger as the royal guard stands either side of the five guards brought in from outside. Lady Christa looks at the messenger and he kneels bowing his head. Lady Christa shakes her hand at the five guards who then remove themselves from the room. The general closely follows and the doors are closed.

"Please stand." The messenger does as instructed and stands. He raises his hand in which he held a scroll,

"This is the message that I have brought for your attention. It is straight from the king my Lady." Lady Christa takes the scroll from his hand and slowly unraveled it. She looks down and reads the writing written by the King himself. It read, 'Lady Christa, greetings from me and my people. I have sent this message in hope that you may take into consideration my proposal which is to follow. For some great time I have watched closely at your progress with your fight against the darkness and by being a neighboring land to you I have watched in awe. Watching and hoping that as servants to the darkness that you would not attack us. In high amazement I thank that you have not. I would like to take this opportunity to explain the only reason for not defending against the darkness is that I was scared for the life of my family and my people. My beloved wife and my only son were slaughtered very recently and I no longer wish to obey the scandalous laws of the darkness. What my pledge to you, Lady Christa and your people is let us unite against the darkness and finally fight for what is right. My eyes have been opened to light and my only wish is to save the lives of many innocent souls like my wife and sons. Please Lady

Christa. Let us join our hands and make it through the everlasting night which has shadowed over us for so long. I give you my full gratitude – Shudae.' Lady Christa rolls the scroll back together. She stands silent thinking deeply. What if this was a trick by the darkness to infiltrate the city or part of a larger plan? She slowly walked back to the thrown and took her seat once again. Looking at the messenger she takes a deep breath,

"I agree with your King and I wish to talk to him more personally about the proposal of becoming united against the darkness. Go back to your king and tell him I wish to see him. He must travel here for if I leave the city of Savon it will be at a greater threat than it already is. Do you understand me?" The messenger nods frantically,

"Yes my Lady. I shall leave at once." The messenger turns and departs from the throne room escorted by two of the royal guard. Lady Christa looks at Lady Catherine,

"I wonder what it is that god has planned for us."

Leon and Dante follow as Binor travels at great speed following the lead of his new captured ally. They halt suddenly when the creature lands its feet upon the ground. They had traveled far to a large uninhabited land. Nothing was stood in the way of a large stretched out flat land. Slightly in the distance could be seen three of the beasts pulling along a body along the ground. Binor returns the creature to its sleeping state magically within the staff as Dante and Leon come up close behind him. Leon looks at the figures in the distance,

"It is now dawn. We have traveled far and fast. At last we have found him. We must move quickly before it may be too late." Straight away they continue to move quickly toward the destination in front of them.

Trilogy of Leon

As they come closer and closer Leon withdraws his sword from his back galloping upon Savior. Dante and Binor fly above him keeping at the same speed. Dante removes a throwing knife from his holster across his chest and throws it toward one of the beasts as a surprise attack. As the knife draws in closer it bursts into many knives and them into even more. At least a hundred blades crash into the back of the beast and as they do so the beast vanishes into a rain of dust. The two hell creatures left drop the limp body of Shione onto the ground and run toward the oncoming threat. The one gives flight to tackle Binor on his dragon as the other jumps and dives for Leon. Dante continues without stopping to the aid of Shione as Binor struggles with the flying creature. His dragon bits at its neck as the creature claws desperately to survive but its attempts prove useless as the dragon rips its body in two. Leon is left below with the beast on top of him. Savior kicks violently and bites as hard as he can at the beast having little effect. Leon builds up all his might and kicks the beast into the air. Perfectly timed Binor gets his dragon into position and it lets out a desecrating stream of flame from the back of its throat. With all the creatures banished they continue to meet with Dante. When they reached him he was sat next to Shione holding him up with his one hand and holding his head up with the other,

"Shione, Shione?" Dante shouted time and time again but there was no reply. Shione sat dreary leaning back and forth. Leon walks over and kneels down in front of him. Looking at him he realizes that Shione is badly beat up and he was in serious concussion. Leon said to the others,

"We need to get him somewhere warm. We need drink and food. I fear that he may have been pushed to his very limits." As they all sat thinking about possible solutions and a quick way of getting him to safety a very small creature stumbles along the ground taking no notice of the four men all around him. It walks daftly straight through the middle of them as they sit watching it stroll by. Binor walks over to the slow moving creature as it continued to walk away and picks it up gently with his hand. He holds his hand out and the creature stood looking at him with dopey eyes. Binor looks over at Leon and Dante,

"We have food for him?" The little creature suddenly seems to awaken and starts looking around waving its stubby little hairy arms in fright. It walks around the edges of Binor's hands and looks over the edge to see how far down it is trying to find a safe way to run away. The creature drops down and sits crossed legged. It laid its head in its hands as if it were sulking. Binor took back from the strange behavior moves his head closer to his hand where the little creature sat. He moved his hand so close that his nose was nearly touching the creature. The creature looks up at Binor and gives him an upset depressed look. Quietly it sighs and as it does announces,

"I hate you." Binor shoots his head back looking overwhelmingly at the creature. He looks dazed from Dante and Leon to the creature and back again.

"Did you hear that? The little thing spoke." Leon and Dante both looked at each other and cracked up in hysterics. Leon stood leaving Dante with Shione and walked over to Binor holding the creature,

Trilogy of Leon

"I haven't known you long friend but I'm really starting to like you." Binor in defense of himself being laughed at replies,

"No Leon, it did really. It said it hates me." Leon put his hand on Binor's shoulder chuckling under his breath. The little tiny creature looks over Binor's shoulder at Leon and with a squeak said,

"I don't know what you're laughing at. Have you seen yourself lately mister?" Leon gob smacked looks at the creature and points at it. Leon looks over at Dante and back at the creature once more,

"The little, the little thing spoke." Binor shakes his head smiling,

"Ha see, I told you it did, didn't I. I knew it." Dante remains speechless looking at the two of them staring amazed at the creature. It spoke once again,

"What's wrong with you two? Have you never seen a small person before?" Leon and Binor just looked at each other not knowing what to say,

"Please may you put me down? I'm not very good with heights you know." Binor kneels down and lets the creature step off his hand. Binor and Leon both take a step back not knowing what to expect from the little creature,

"My name is Clemmentina. Your not going to eat me are you mister? Please don't eat me. I wouldn't be yummy because look I'm really hairy and I wouldn't be much of a meal." Leon kneels down on both knees and looks down at the little creature,

"So Clemmentina, may I ask what your doing out here in the middle of nowhere? And no, don't worry we wont eat you." The tiny creature relaxes and sits down on the ground. It smiles a large smile and replies to Leon question,

"I am collecting beans. For my collection, look" the creature reaches into its hair and pulls out its hand opening it wide. Leon moves as close as he could to try and see the items which should have been in the creatures hands. Puzzled Leon asks,

"I am very sorry but I cannot see anything in your hand." The creature frowns,

"How can you not see? You must be very blind mister. There humongous and there really heavy to. They have a special use but I'm not going to tell you what it is because it's a secret." Leon looks up at Binor who stood scratching his head still trying to get to grips with the little creature. The creature continues to speak,

"So I told you my name now you have to tell me yours and his and that man and that man." She said as she pointed at Dante, Shione and Binor. Leon points at himself and then the others as he explains,

"I'm Leon. This big man is Binor. The man over there in the black is Dante and the other man is Shione. What sort of creature are you?" In reply the creature proudly pronounces,

"I am a Hitancois Tanadrian Liperdrainious." Leon raises his eyebrows,

"That's a very long and complicated thing to say. I won't ask you to repeat it. Here, it must have taken you days to travel this far across this land?" Clemmentina shakes her head smiling cheekily,

"Nope, It hasn't even took me a day so far Mister Leon. You see when the big light goes away and the little light appears that is a day. But that's only one hour for me

Trilogy of Leon

and my kind." Leon tries to figure out the time it may of took for the creature to get this far but gave up,

"Okay then. How have you survived this long?" Clemmytina raises a finger to her lips,

"Don't tell anybody mister but it's the beans. The red ones are my food and the green ones are my drink. There are other ones to." Leon smiles knowing exactly what to ask next,

"Would your beans be any help to us Clemmytina?" She looks at the others and back,

"Yes they will be mister because they are magic with the blessing of the earth and there special and its up to me and my friends to collect them because that's why we are alive." Leon slightly confused puts on a friendly face,

"Please may we have a couple for my friend Shione because he is injured quite badly and if he doesn't have any he could possibly die?" Clemmytina looks over at Shione still sitting dazed next to Dante,

"I think your friend needs a purple one. If I give you a purple one would you take me wherever you're going please because I've been lonely and you're my friend? You wouldn't leave a poor little helpless lady out here all alone open for danger would you Mister Leon sir?" Leon put out his hand and Clemmytina stepped onto it as Leon stood up. Clemmytina bobbled up and down in excitement as they walked over to Shione. Leon put his hand next to Shione mouth as Dante held him up with his head back. Clemmytina reaches deep into her hair pockets and pulled her hand out clinched together as if there were something inside of her fist. Leon with his other hand opened Shione's mouth slightly and Clemmytina reached over the edge of Leon's hand letting go of the clinch of her fist. She watched as something only she could see fell into his mouth,

"Close his mouth and makes sure he swallows into his tummy." Leon closes his mouth and holds his mouth closed until Shione coughed slightly. Dante let him sit back as Leon stood up properly with Clemmytina still in his hand. Binor walks over,

"Did it work?" Clemmytina looks over at puts her hands on her waist. After giving him a frown she said,

"I see you must be mister impatient then." Binor crossed his arms raising his head looking down on Clemmytina taking offence from getting bad attitude from such a small source. Shione starts to shake slightly and he opens his eyes. Looking around he smiles,

"I've got to get me some of them. There great. What was it?" Clemmytina smiles and shuffles her waist from left to right,

"That was a purple one mister Shione." Shione stands looking strangely at the creature. He looks at Leon and glances to Dante and then to Binor,

"Well isn't this a surprise. I haven't seen you Dante or Binor in to long a time. It's good to see you and Leon. Good to see you in good shape." Shione looks down at Clemmytina,

"And you little one, I have you to thank for my swift recovery." Shione looks around at the four companions. He puts his one hand on Dante's shoulder and the other on Leon's,

"Thank you for coming to find me. I trust with you all being here the city and Lady Christa and Catherine are fine and in good health." Leon sighs in relieve,

"Indeed Shione, indeed they are." They all continue to speak and catch up before deciding to make tracks back to the city from the way in which they had came. All together they began to travel side by side. Shione rode on the back of Dante's dragon with Dante and Clemmytina as promised traveled with Leon upon Shione as Binor traveled alone beside them.

Emperor Glenthoron stands looking out into the day. He wore as always a long black cloak. A helmet covered his face at all time. The shiny silver shape of the helmet matched the shape of a dragons head. He carried a long staff with him which was twirled in shape. At the top of the staff was a black jewel being held up by three arms. He looked out over his large city which remained darkened by low clouds in the sky. Fires burnt throughout the city. The city was named Septhune and was once a thriving city of traders and was a much loved place. There was no meaning to this city anymore apart from to generate weapons of all magical expense and to breed hellish creatures like those which attacked the City of Savon. A small ugly goblin like creature steps up limping behind Glenthoron,

"Master, I have news." Glenthoron turned and looked at his slave,

"continue." He muttered under his breath,

"The attack on the city was a failure master. The beasts were all slain." Glenthoron growls angrily,

"Did they manage to escape with anything of any value?" the little goblin shakes his head,

"No master. Shione was rescued by a couple of men and they left on there way back to the city." Glenthoron lashes out and hits the goblin sending him shooting to the floor. He raises his hand and lifts the goblin with his magic,

"This is not good news. I do not wish to receive bad news from you useless slaves." He drops his spell sending the goblin once again crashing to the floor. He walks over to a large throne built from strong iron. Sitting down on the throne he points at the goblin and snarls,

"You, go personally. Take the Beuthis, all of them. Also take all of the Henais. Don't bother showing your face again if you don't succeed." The goblin gathers himself to his feet,

"But master. That is over ten thousand of our forces can we afford to take such a risk?" Rising to his feet Glenthoron jolts his staff forward sending a small blast through the air sending the goblin flying across the room. The goblin hits the side of the wall and lands with a thump crawling into a ball to protect itself from any further abuse,

"I want that city to be destroyed don't you understand the importance? I need that jewel from that wretched woman and she needs to burn upon a stake. I want every single soul within those city walls to scream in pain and agony as they fall into the depths of hell. I am the king of the land. I am the master of the heavens and hell. This earth will be mine and nobody will stand before me." Glenthoron shouts loudly while snarling and growling. His self confidence and determination, pushing him to any means necessary. His aim was to become the ultimate leader of all the lands. The goblin jumps up and keeps his head down while running to the door. It takes one look back,

Trilogy of Leon

"Yes master. I am sorry master. I shall see to it at once." With this the goblin exited the room as Glenthoron returned to his seat on the throne. A man walks from the shadows in the corner of the room. His hands held behind his back and his posture at a high. He wore a fall body gown with a hood covering his face. The man raises his head in which the light lit part of his face. The side of the face which had been lit was covered in scars and grazes and his eye was missing. In its place was a fake eye with an oval red mark in the centre,

"Master, I believe you under estimate the power of these individuals aiding the Lady Christa as I once did. My advice would be to send everything at once to crush the city in one large sweep." Glenthoron raises his hand as a sign to stop the stranger from speaking. He looks at him from the tops of his eyes as his head is down. With the evil stare he replies,

"You have lost one battle against these inferior pests Lord Thain. If you don't keep your opinions to yourself then you won't get the chance to fight another."

It was late afternoon as the travelers reached back at the city of Savon the gates had been successfully restored and improved in terms of defense power. The gates are opened as Lord Shione, Dante and Binor enter on foot with the Dragons sitting calmly outside either side of the gates. Leon strolled in on the back of Savior with Clemmytina holding onto the reigns sitting comfortably and stable. As they had a look around the city on the way to the palace they saw that the clean up of the city had been taken under way quite well and the city was nearly back to how it once was.

Estaban Bridges

Within the palace they all meet in the throne room. Lady Christa hugs Lord Shione tightly glad to have him back unharmed. Clemmytina was introduced to Lady Christa and Catherine as they all sat around a large table. They spoke like a true family and all was warm and caring. Leon spoke about his life as did Lady Catherine as they all listened in interest. Hope had been restored to these souls sitting in the room and Clemmytina enjoyed the company of her new found friends. The time quickly passed by and each of the individuals decided to make tracks. Fairly tired Lady Catherine leaves to her room to sleep taking Clemmytina with her. Dante and Binor retreated to the depths of the city pubs to drown there sorrows and to get merry in time of need. Leon decided to also leave to his room thinking about how good he felt and how much strength he could feel within himself. He thought strongly that maybe he hadn't yet found the true power within himself that the gods may have blessed him with. He lay down to sleep as Lord Shione and Lady Christa remained in the throne room. They had spoken long and in depth as close friends instead of in the way of authority. It was all quite personnel as they sat and laughed together smiling and having great feelings of care for each other. The night continues to pass as the stay awake talking about the beauty of the stars and the clear night sky.

Birds tweet and sing merrily as Leon awakens from a deep sleep. He stretches and takes a long deep breath. He looks out of the window to see the sun gleaming bright in the sky without a cloud in sight. He dresses and leaves his room walking through the long corridors of the palace. From behind he heard a quiet voice,

Trilogy of Leon

"Good afternoon mister Leon." He turned to find Clemmytina walking close behind him pulling slightly on his trouser leg. He smiles and gently picks her up,

"How are you Clemmytina? Did you sleep well?" She gives a slow single nod smiling,

"Yes I did indeed thank you very much mister Leon. Where are you going" Leon shrugged his shoulders,

"I'm not to sure myself. Where are the others?" Clemmytina pointed the way toward the front door of the palace,

"They all went to meet mister King." Leon raises an eyebrow,

"Let's go see what is happening then shall we?" Leon began to walk to the exit of the palace to meet the others at the city gates.

At the city of Darkness, Septhune the ultimate attack force of hell creatures was being prepared. Emperor Glenthoron placed the orders for the attack to happen as quick as could be done and so had began a magic operation to open portals which in turn would give the chance for the enemy forces to go through the portals leading the literally outside of the City of Savon. As the rules of magic went the portals could not be opened in the territory occupied by any light magic because there was a barrier preventing it from doing so. The portals would be connected just outside of the City of Savon next to the moat surrounding the city. Emperor Glenthoron set up the battle plan that all of the force would enter the portals getting into a set formation on the other side in ready terms for the battle. Lord Thain would be assisting in the battle and so would use his magic force to solidify the moat making it much easier for the darkness army to

Estaban Bridges

cross instead of having to cross the moat. The plans were well under way and all the forces began to get into place waiting for further orders from Glenthoron himself. At the temple of darkness Emperor Glenthoron sat with Lord Thain discussing the situation,

"Thain, I know that you are very useless at eliminating such an easy thereat but I revived you for a reason and that is for you to get rid of the threat at hand. I have issued you with more power than you have ever had. You will not disappoint me this time. Do you understand?" Thain smiles on one side of his face,

"You do not understand my master. You have not seen the power that these humans possess. If you were to come with us and witness the mighty strength of these individuals then you would be took back by shock yourself." Glenthoron laughs out loud,

"There is nobody and no set of humans who can be more powerful than me Thain. The Lord, the king of hell himself has issued me with his own power to overcome the stupidity of such people. If I was not mistaken Thain, I would say you were afraid." Thain stands and walks away with his back turned to Glenthoron. With anger and spite he replies,

"If I did not know the power you possess master and if I were more foolish than I may be I would take your head from your body and hold it high in my hand." Glenthoron jumps from his seat and walks over behind Thain,

"How dare you threaten me you incompetent fool? I bring you back from the deep depths of hell itself and this is how you repay me. I should desecrate you with the touch of my hand while you stand there thinking such things." Thain walks slowly and calmly further away and reaches the door to the room,

"I may be following your orders Glenthoron but I am not a slave to you and I never will be. I will carry out this attack upon Savon out of hatred and revenge. Not for the pleasure of your greed." With this Thain leaves the room slamming the door behind him. Glenthoron was left standing feeling hatred against Thain and wanting to reduce him to nothing more than a small weak pile of dust. In stead he calmly hobbles over to a small crystal ball sat upon a small stand next to the throne and places his hands on it while whispering,

"Sarahleene appear before me. Show yourself and appear before me." The crystal ball begins to glow as Glenthoron removes his hands and takes a step back. A large black flash suddenly fills the room and Glenthoron stands looking at a short woman kneeling in front of the crystal ball on in its stand. The woman had very long straight black hair with perfectly covered black eyes. Although she was short she had a large chest and she wore a tight black outfit. Her boots were high heel going up just below her knees and half her face was covered with a black mask. She looks up at Glenthoron and smiles a cheeky smile while tilting her head to her side. As she rose to her feet she moved closer to Glenthoron and placed her arms around his shoulders while slowly walking around circling him. She moves close to his ear and begins to whisper in a quiet cute voice,

"You summon me master but yet you seem worried and disturbed. What can her mistress do to be of service to her master?" Glenthoron grasps her hand and pulls her in front of him. He holds her face with a hand gently

Estaban Bridges

on either cheek. He smiles and kisses her softly on the forehead,

"My dear Sarahleene, I need you to do me such a big favor and follow Thain. Once he has completed or once he has failed to complete the extermination I have set him on his course to do I need you, I need you to slowly pull his heart from within his body and bring it to me. Make sure he dies a painful death. Understand that if you fail to do so you will end up with similar sacrifice of life." Sarahleene smiles and kisses Glenthoron on the cheek,

"I will not fail master. I would not dream of doing such a thing." With this she clicks her fingers and disappears in a small twister of smoke. Emperor Glenthoron runs his hand across his chin in stress and looks up to the roof shaking his head. He walks over to his throne and drops himself down while letting out a mild sigh.

Leon walks slowly to the city gates to find Lady Christa and the others standing with a large man. Behind him was a small team of around twenty soldiers all armed and on horseback. Leon walks over behind Shione and listened to the conversation. Lady Christa talks calmly with the man who Leon presumed to be King Shudae.

"You travel from your land to speak to me about becoming one with my peoples but yet up until just three or four days ago you were under the thumb of evil? How would you feel if this was the other way round Shudae?" The King, slightly nods his head,

"I fully understand your concern Christa but as I have said before I wish and my people wish to be free once again. We want to be able to live in love and care for each other instead of being made to slaughter and fight against what we believe in. you and the people of the City of Savon have returned hope to us once again and we wish to grab our freedom with all our strength." King Shudae drops slowly down to one knee while keeping eye contact with Lady Christa. He withdraws his sword and holds it lay across both hands. Lowering his head and looking to the ground he lifts his arms and offers Lady Christa his sword,

"Please Lady Christa. Take my sword and take my people. Take them under your wings to fight for what is right. I shall stand down from my throne and nobody will sit in my place other than you. I will make this sacrifice for the sake of my people, for the sake of light." Lady Christa takes a small step back away from where the king was kneeling. She moves her hand in such a gesture as to tell the king to rise to his feet. He looks up and thinking the worst steps back up still holding the sword in his hands. Lady Christa remains speechless and the king sighs while returning the sword back into its holster. Lady Christa walks forward and places one hand on the kings shoulder,

"We will unite King Shudae of the Shangerian people. We will fight the darkness until our souls are drained from the bodies in which we own. I do not wish to strip you of your throne or your people." The king smiled and becomes delighted with the news. The soldiers behind him on horseback all shout and cheer loudly and Lady Christa smiles. The entire large group of people at the city gates feels even more hope had been introduced and the all began to celebrate. Lady Christa announces that a dinner shall be held in the Palace hall for the King and his men and Lady Christa and her companions.

Estaban Bridges

News spread quickly around the City of Savon and the city folk came to the palace and gathered at the city gates to try to catch a glimpse of the new allies. The whole city became engulfed in excitement and joy. As the day went on the night began to set in as they continued to celebrate.

Late afternoon King Shudae sat in the palace hall with Lady Christa, Catherine, Shione, Leon, Dante, Binor and Clemmytina. They all drank city wine apart from Clemmytina who could not stand the taste. They had already been properly introduced and many question and answers had been exchanged between them all. King Shudae learnt about how certain battles had taken place and how they had all got together. The others had learnt how the King had given into the darkness to save the lives of his family and his peoples but they had been abused from the start. The last straw was the Kings son and wife being killed in cold blood. The King knew some important information which in later times could prove useful. One main worry on the Kings mind was what would happen once the Darkness found out about the treaty between the two Cities. The king spoke worryingly,

"Lady Christa. I am afraid about the safety of my city and the people within. Once the darkness find out that our two lands have joined together they will try to break us in two. In which I believe they will go for the weaker of the two of us which further more is my people and my city." Lady Christa looks around at the rest of the people around the table,

"How many soldiers do you hold in your city Shudae?" The king takes a second to think,

"I have around ten thousand men available to fight for the city. This is including the younger men and a few men from the land surrounding the city." Lady Christa also takes a second to think,

"In what condition are your men may I ask?" Shudae smirks,

"Since being under the orders of darkness they have become fat and idle Lady Christa. They may not even be up to fighting the darkness the way in which they would have been able to." Lady Christa glances over at Dante and Binor,

"Shudae, will you except help from two of my closest friends?" The king also glances over looking at where Lady Christa had just looked,

"I would indeed. It would be of great help." Lady Christa stands from her seat and walks over between Dante and Binor sitting side by side. She puts her arms around each of them and pulls them closer to her,

"Binor and Dante, please help King Shudae train his men to some sort of exceptional standard without taking any time to slack." Dante and Binor both look at each other. Both of them liking the idea of becoming generals in there own way. Smiling they both jump to there feet,

"It would be a great challenge my Lady. We shall train them to be soldiers worthy of your appraisal." Dante waits for Binor's reply,

"Yes my Lady. We won't disappoint you." Lady Christa pats them both gently on their backs and walks back over to Shudae.

"Theirs no time to waste, you better hurry because as we all know news travels fast over the land." The king rises to his feet and strolls over to Christa side of the table. He kisses her softly on the cheek,

"Thank you Christa. I will make sure that this day goes down in our history as a great day for my people. I shall see you soon." He begins to walk toward the door out of the hall as did Dante and Binor. The king turns the rest of them sitting at the table,

"It's been a great pleasure meeting you all and I hope we will meet again soon. Take care." Leon and Shione slightly lower there heads in slight bow to the King. Clemmytina waves frantically just incase he was not able to see and Lady Catherine smiles while playing with her hair. Dante, Binor and King Shudae leave the room and travel to the palace doors. Dante talks to the king as they walk,

"You're going to enjoy the ride." Shudae looks over confused,

"I'm sorry I do not understand Dante. How do you mean enjoy the ride?" Dante smile and his eyes widen,

"The ride back to your city, on my dragon." The king stops and looks worryingly at Dante and Binor,

"You mean, those dragons outside the gates were your dragons?" They both nod smiling,

"And you ride on the back of those things?" They both continue to nod,

"You want me to ride on the back of one of those things with you?" Dante continues to nod as Binor's grin becomes larger,

"He's scared Dante." Dante hits the king on the shoulder,

"You will be fine. I've only fallen off the gal about twelve times." The king's mouth drops,

Trilogy of Leon

"Fallen, fallen off?" Dante and Binor continue to walk as the King stands feeling quite vulnerable. He begins to jog after them to catch them up,

"I've got to ride back with my soldiers. I can't leave them to ride alone." Without stopping Binor replies,

"Don't worry about them Shudae. They have all fallen asleep already with all that ale they've drank." The king sighs and slumps his shoulders as they continue on there way.

Lady Christa sits back down at the table. Left remaining were Leon, Shione, Clemmytina and Lady Catherine. Lady Catherine spoke with Clemmytina as the others spoke together,

"Clemmytina, you make me wonder. How many of your people are there?" Clemmytina smiles and sits down on the table in front of Catherine,

"There are many of us. Yes lots and lots and lots but we hide and nobody can find us." Catherine smiles and tickles Clemmytina gently with her finger,

"How old are you if you do not mind me asking?" Counting on her fingers she replies,

"In your years I am one hundred and" She pauses, "three." Catherine gasps,

"Oh my, that is old isn't it?" Clemmytina sighs depressingly,

"It is much older than that in my time. I am actually very old." Clemmytina reached into one of her hair pockets and pulls out her hand. Upon opening her fist she says,

"Would you like a bean Miss Catherine? This one is one of the special ones." Catherine shakes her hand,

"No thank you Clemmytina I am quite alright but I will take you up on your offer another time." Sadly

Clemmytina returned the bean into her little hair pocket,

"That's to bad Miss Catherine because that one was an orange one." She steps up on the table and waves at Catherine. She began to walk over to Lady Christa sitting with Shione and Leon. Lady Catherine stands,

"Goodnight Mother, goodnight brother. Goodnight Shione and Clemmytina. I shall see you in the morning. I hope you sleep well." The others said goodnight to Catherine and she left the room. Clemmytina listened into the conversation between the three others now left in the room. Shione scratched his chin,

"But my Lady, if what you predict is true then how will we be able to keep up our defense?" Leon interrupted,

"Such a thing may never happen so why should we get so worked up about it at such an early stage?" Shione raised his voice and continued,

"Its better to think ahead of such difficulties Leon or else we will be unprepared." Lady Christa stood. Leon and Shione both fell silent,

"If what I predict is true then the darkness will send an overwhelming force to penetrate our city walls. We are highly vulnerable as we stand here waiting for something to happen and therefore we have to be one step ahead. We need to flee the city." Shione huffed and pushed him self away from the table. He stood and began to pace back and forth,

"I am sorry for speaking openly My Lady but we cannot just pack our bags and run as if we have no chance." Leon also rose to his feet,

Trilogy of Leon

"If it is safe to do so then we must for the good of the people of the city and to keep us all safe." Christa looked to her feet in deep thought,

"If we left they would come straight for us and in any term we have nowhere we can go with there being so many of us. We must remember it's not just us anymore it's the Shangerian people we have to think of to" Leon shakes his head,

"If they come here then they can help fortify the city, surely." Shione once again huffs,

"This will still make no difference with so many darkness forces against us. We need something big. We need enough soldiers to cover the land around the city. Enough to make an unbreakable wall." The three of them stop arguing and stand motionless and speechless. Clemmytina walked to the edge of the table and sat herself down dangling her feet of the side. She looks at them each individually and eventually let out a quiet little laugh,

"You are all silly boys and girls" The three of them look and frown at Clemmytina, she shrugs her small shoulders,

"There are such easy answers to such easy questions." Lady Christa takes interest and kneels in front of the table looking at Clemmytina. Softly she asks,

"Please explain to us what you're thinking." Clemmytina rolls her eyes,

"You want to move away so you can be safer yes?" Christa nods,

"But you want to still put up a fight yes?" Again she nods,

"Well the smart thing to do is move away from here and hide. Then come back again bigger and better as a big surprise." Christa shakes her head slightly,

"Unfortunately Clemmytina, that isn't going to work. We won't be able to find anywhere to hide and they will come straight after us." Clemmytina smiles,

"I know where you could hide Miss Christa." Christa stands and picks Clemmytina from off the table and sits her softly onto her other hand,

"And where is that then?" Clemmytina makes the movements as if she were swimming in water and then sits back still smiling,

"What do you mean?" Christa asks not fully getting the physical explanation,

"What I mean is everybody should hide where you can't be seen unless that person looking for you has a boat or can fly like a bird." Christa turns facing Leon and Shione as they pay close attention to the possible successful idea but Christa questions further,

"I am sorry to keep asking questions but how do we know that there is anything or anywhere we can stay out in the ocean. If we go too far we would come across a distant land and that is one thing we do not wish to do." Clemmytina replies,

"You would not come across a distant land you would come across the legendary Sea city, Seeyarta. This would just be a stop for you as you get ready in preparation to return to your own land. To reclaim what is rightfully yours." Shione steps forward,

"I have heard many stories from sailors and travelers. They spoke of this city, The City of Seeyarta but it is known as a myth. A fairy tale for sailors to send there kids

Trilogy of Leon

to sleep when they return home." Clemmytina places her head in her hands smiling,

"And Mister Shione, what have you heard in these stories?" Shione takes a moment to recall,

"I have heard that the City is built on the sea bed in the sea between this land and the next. I've heard the sea surrounds it as if it were not there. It is impossible to find unless you have a Seeyarta Pearl. Also many ships and boats have disappeared, vanished when they've gone to where the city is apparently built. That is just the beginning." Clemmytina sighs loudly looking up at the ceiling,

"What else have you heard about it?" Shione continues,

"I've heard it's a city of paradise. Darkness has never set foot in such a place let alone known about such a place. Everybody who lives there, lives in love and happiness, once you've been their, you never wish to leave." Clemmytina jumps up to her feet,

"Yep that's pretty much exactly right. Paradise Miss Christa and I've been there." Christa shocked replies,

"You have been there? Such a place exists? How is that possible?" Clemmytina gives a quick explanation,

"Well, I was collecting beans and I came across an elderly man, very friendly. We became friends and he took me to his home, Seeyarta. Before he unfortunately passed away he gave me his pearl and told me to go on many journeys and so that's what I did. The whole city is magic and that's how it is able to be where it is. It is so secret and so perfect." Lady Christa places Clemmytina back on the table and sits down where she was at before. She thought long and hard,

"What makes you think they would welcome us Clemmytina and with such a large amount of people surely we could not take everybody?" Clemmytina puts her hands behind her head and leans back. Relaxing on the table she declares in great honor,

"I am Clemmytina the specially chosen, one of only a few, Princess' of Seeyarta. The elderly man was the son of the late King of Seeyarta and made me one of the princess' because I stayed by his side and gave him many beans. He said I was like a daughter to him. I'm special, your not." Christa smiles as do Leon and Shione,

"Is that right?" Clemmytina sits up,

"Yes, yes it is. I am. I'm not lying. Really, I'm telling the truth." Shione questions,

"Who is the ruler at this time and is there enough room for all of our peoples?"

"The ruler at the present time Mister Shione is King Livorus. The answer to your other question is there's more room down there than you think there is." Leon, Shione and Christa remain staring at Clemmytina deciding whether to take her seriously or think she was playing a game with them. Christa decided she wanted to speak to Clemmytina alone,

"Shione, Leon, would you mind if I and Clemmytina could have some privacy please?" Taking the hint Shione bows his head to Lady Christa,

"As you wish Christa, I shall go to rest. Sleep well and I shall be over in the morning." Christa smiles and Shione leaves the room. Leon steps over and kisses Lady Christa softly on her hand,

"Whatever decision you make mother will be the right decision. Sleep well and you Clemmytina." Leon proceeds to leave the room as Clemmytina waves. Once the room became empty Christa looked seriously at Clemmytina,

"Has what you've told us today been the truth Clemmytina, nothing but the truth?" Clemmytina places a hand on her chest,

"I promise Miss Christa that it is the truth and I'm just trying to help because you're my friends and friends take care of each other and help each other. I like all of you lots and lots and you're all really nice to me. I don't want to see any of you get hurt Miss Christa because that would make me really upset. You're not going to get hurt in any way are you?" Christa smiles and runs her finger over the top of Clemmentina's head,

"Don't worry, were be just fine and I'm going to make sure your just fine to." Clemmytina grabs hold to Christa's finger and places a kiss on her finger tip.

"The pearl of mine is hidden Miss Christa but I can get it straight away with my only white bean." Christa stands and places Clemmytina on her hand. As she walks toward the door she says with the softest voice,

"All in time Clemmytina, now we will get our rest." They continue to Christa's bedroom to rest for the next day.

The sun rises and breaks its light through the clouds which covered the sky. It was a warm morning and it all seemed calm. The city folk had risen cheerfully and began there daily tasks. All was peaceful within the city. From afar rain clouds could be seen showing possible bad weather heading the city's way.

Orders had been made from Lady Christa that the sharpest and finest weapons in the city should be collected in one space. The blacksmiths were all ordered to make new armor of great strength using the best material that could be found while other blacksmiths made new weapons to make up for the old useless ones. The women in the city were asked to make many new cloths for all the people. Everybody in the city had an important job to do and they were all happy to do the jobs which would help the escape to safety.

Lady Christa stood at the window in her room looking out over the city. She saw all her people rushing around the city happily going about there tasks. She thought to herself about what she wanted to succeed and how she wanted these people to live a life without any fear and without the constant thought of a possible attack taking place at any given time. She wished to herself that one day her daughter could rule over the people with no troubles and no worries. She wished to herself for perfection. What she wished for was heaven on earth.

Shione knocked on Christa's door and she invited him in,

"You called for me Christa?" She turned and took a deep breath,

"Shione, were going. I have issued the orders for everybody to get prepared. I have sent a message to Shudae to bring all his people to the city. We will all leave here in the next few days once they arrive." Shione sits down on a chair up against the wall,

"Are you sure this is what you wish to do Christa. It must be a difficult decision for you?" Christa sighed some what ashamed of her decision,

"It is for the best of the souls which live around us Shione. My plan is that we get to the City of Seeyarta and stay there for as long as it takes. Then we shall come back

Trilogy of Leon

to this, my city. We shall be back and live as we do but without the constant threat of danger." Shione leans his head against the wall,

"There is so much we have to accomplish to get to our goal Christa. Is there enough hope to drag us through?" Christa smile a soft small smile,

"As long as there's good people like you Shione then there shall always be hope." Shione huffs smiling,

"Christa, people like you, Leon, Catherine and the others are what give me my hope. Together we can keep each others hope alive. Together we will survive." Christa turns her back and as she was before she looks out of the window. Shione questions,

"Christa, where will we get the means to cross the sea to find Seeyarta?"

"We will travel to the river further down stream. The riders have returned with news that there is a small port on the river bank overfilling of large ships. They have told me there are enough ships there to hold the biggest of all armies. What shall happen is we will march into the port and take these ships." Shione frowns not entirely impressed by the plan,

"And how do we know this will actually work? Why is there so many ships just sitting there? Where are all the crewmen of the ships? Have you thought about these things?" Christa remaining at the window and gives out a quiet giggle,

"Shione, you make me laugh. You're always so guarding. I am not as delicate as I used to be. I have thought and questioned those things. It will work because it is a small port overwhelmed with ships. The ships are sitting there unused because the darkness have not got

Estaban Bridges

the resources to travel across the ocean, this is because of there attack to the North and that's where all the crewmen are. It is the perfect opportunity to take the ships and flee while the forces are being held up elsewhere." Shione stands and opens the door,

"Looks to me like you have all possible routes covered My Lady. I shall help with the preparation." He leaves the room closing the door firmly behind him. Christa sits down on her bed and thinks about is she actually doing what is right. Her mind and heart, her soul and her body being pulled in separate directions. Which is the right direction to take, she wonders as she remained sitting in a dazed dream.

Emperor Glenthoron walks with Lord Thain through the dark fiery streets of the Darkness city, Septhune. They stop walking when they came across a formatted large army. Looking through the ranks Glenthoron speaks clearly to Thain,

"I have decided that I shall be coming through the portals with you and the army Thain. I want to make sure this all happens properly."

"What about the struggle to the North? So many of those tiny creatures but yet so much havoc caused. Won't you assist there?" Glenthoron shakes his head,

"I don't know what the problem is. All I have heard is that there's little creatures covered in hair. It makes me seriously think how stupid and worthless these creatures standing before me are." Thain takes a step forward,

"Maybe it's just the leader they take orders from." Thain continues to walk looking at all the beasts lined in blocks of a hundred by a hundred. With two separate groups of five rows by five rows. Altogether the army consisted of around two hundred and fifty thousand beasts and soldiers. Emperor Glenthoron remained where he stood thinking angrily to himself. If he didn't need Thain so badly to govern over the troops he would have killed him himself by now. Nevertheless he remembered about Sarahleene who was waiting for the right time to follow out her orders. He grinned to himself and followed after Thain.

It was morning and Dante and Binor had arrived at the City of Shangedain with King Shudae. It was a fairly sized city but seemed run down and almost as if it had been forgotten. Shudae walks to the front gates and looks over confused at Dante and Binor,

"I don't understand. We should have been met or at least questions by the guards." Dante walks over beside Shudae,

"Well where's the welcoming party?" Shudae steps closer to the city gates and knocks on them loudly. A voice comes from behind,

"Who goes there?" Shudae moves his head closer to the gates,

"The king idiot, Open the gates." A small hatch opens in the one side of the large gates and an eye peers over. Upon seeing Dante and Shudae standing in front of the gates the hatch closes and the gates begin to open. A soldier walks out and bows his head to the king,

"I am sorry sir but since you've been gone we went on high alert just incase. When we saw those beasts sir we didn't know what to do. Glad to have you back sir." Binor walks over and follows Dante and Shudae into the grounds of the city. Inside the city walls it was untidy and dirty. Many people sat around on the floor or on barrels drinking or eating. The city was in bad shape and so were the people. Dante halts Shudae,

"Where are the soldiers Shudae?" He raises his arms and twirls himself slowly around,

"The people you see before you are just a selection of them Dante." Binor laughs loudly,

"These men are not soldiers. These are idle beggars." Shudae looks down to his feet,

"Ever since the darkness took over my city it has become less and less respectable as did the people. I am ashamed to say that I am the king of this." Dante looks around again,

"Shudae, How come the soldiers you rode in with had uniforms and looked generally well trained and taken care of?" Shudae lightens up,

"Ah, my royal guard Dante. I have around a thousand of them at my service. They have all stayed loyal to me over the hard times and have stayed the way they once were. These men I am truly proud of." Dante steps forward,

"We have to work fast and hard. Gather your soldiers Shudae." The awakening of the Shangerian troops was to become under way. Dante and Binor took the full responsibility of getting the soldiers into the right frame of mind ant to battle standards. Little did they know that as they spoke a rider was on his way with the news of the evacuation of the two cities?

Early afternoon Lady Christa sat quietly and alone in the throne room trying to figure out in her head her future steps to make. Shione entered and stood looking at Lady Christa with a strange look upon his face which Christa had never really seen before. She stepped down from the throne and took a few small steps forward,

"What is wrong Shione?" Shione looks across slightly away from her so that he had no eye contact,

"I strongly believe you are doing the wrong thing Christa. Since our conversation this morning I have done nothing apart from think about all the different problems we face." Christa remained silent,

"What I mean is there are so many things that can go wrong for us. What if we are about to leave and Emperor Glenthoron throws an attack upon us? Or even as we speak we are attacked? What then? We are and will be unprepared for such a thing." Christa changes the subject,

"Shione, when was the last time that you could just sit? When was the last time, any of us could just sit without a worry in the world? It has been so long that I cannot remember such a time. Wouldn't you love to give anything to be able to calmly sit in a calm and happy trance, without one worry on your mind?" Shione shakes his head,

"No Christa I would not. Not if that means laying down my responsibilities and fleeing from the very thing we are fighting against. Not if that means running away from everything I have fought so hard to protect and keep as my own. Not if it means giving up hope because that makes me nothing better than the darkness themselves." Christa raised her voice as she replied,

"I am not fleeing as you think I am Shione. If anything I am giving the people hope. You cannot say that what I have chosen to do is a bad thing Shione." in instant reaction Shione shouts back,

"You say your decision is giving the people hope but at what excessive cost? At what dam sacrifice are you making to give hope, when the same hope can be kept staying as we are? I cannot say that your decision is a good thing neither a bad but I feel you are making the wrong decision Christa. Open you eyes and see the light. This time you are wrong and you remain wrong." Christa in rage walks hurriedly over to where Shione stood. She pulled her arm back and suddenly slapped him with her full strength. As she hit his face his head got knocked sideways. As he looked back at her she stepped back and said furiously,

"Remember your place Shione. You have no right to speak to me in that manner. Your place is by my side to protect me and serve for me not to criticize me. Understood Shione?" He looked down shaking his head slightly. He removed his sword from by his side and dropped it down on the floor. He lifted his head up high and took a tall stance,

"I have no place here. Not any longer." Christa became confused. Shione continued.

"I strip myself from my duties Lady Christa. I hope your decision works out a success." With this Shione turned and approached the doors to leave. Lady Christa shouts shocked and upset,

"So that's it? You're just going to walk away and leave us? After everything we've been through your going to run away?" Shione turned and shouted disheartened back,

"After everything we've been through you decide to treat me as a worthless slave? After everything we've been through, you of all people should know to treat me better. I returned your son to you Christa. I have helped fight for your city and for the fight against the darkness. I have done nothing but been there for you and support you. I have done everything you have asked of me in the past and it ends like this. It ends with you forgetting where my loyalties lye. I am not the one running away, it is you who is running away." Shione turned and continued toward the doors. Without Christa saying a word he opened the door. He takes one final look back through the throne room at Christa. The moment for them both seemed to become slow. Thoughts flying through each of there minds, strong heated feelings shooting through each of there hearts. Years of being together and being there for each other seemed to be shredded as if it were nothing. Years of the two of them being nothing but as if they were a couple, were to be thrown away as easy as that, as easy as just having a small over exaggerated argument. In one swift movement Shione looked away and closed the door of the throne room He closed the door on his past. Closed the door on Lady Christa and closed the door on the people of the city. Christa began to step forward shouting out to Shione, her voice full of despair and sadness,

"Shione, Shione" She shouted as her eyes filled with tears as they had done many times before,

"Please Shione come back, Shione" She hit the sword lying on the floor gently as she stepped forward. Tears pouring from here eyes she dropped to her knees. In sadness and in hurt she sobbed as she placed her head in her hands. Quietly she tries to shout but was reduced to nothing more than a tearful whisper,

"Come back, come back. I need you." Falling further to the ground she placed her hands on the floor and placed her head also against the floor. Eventually she rolled on to the floor clutching the only thing she had physically left of Shione. Broken and in despair she continued to try and shout but for nobody to hear,

"Please, I love you." Remaining huddled up on the floor her heart broke apart as her dreams shattered like broken glass. She had such high hopes for her and Shione which had now vanished due to his departure from her life. As she bled inside of herself and cried her unhopeful tears Shione continued his way out of the palace. Without stopping he left the palace and traveled down the steps, without speaking or acknowledging any body that he passed. Jumping onto his horse he rode straight to the city gates which were opened for him when he approached. Without looking back as if he did not care he rode out further away from Christa. Across the drawbridge and further into the distance he rode until he could not be seen any longer. Before he got to the forest he stopped and looked at the city from afar. Quietly to himself he whispered encouragingly,

"To the North I ride. I may well see you there my friends." Continuing on his journey he rode into the forest engulfed in its deepness and darkness. Not to be seen again? Only time can tell.

Christa remained in her room in the palace for the rest of the day in remembrance of what she and Shione had been through over the years. Anybody who knocked on the door she called away not wanting to be disturbed. Night came and night passed as morning approached. Leon, Lady Catherine and Clemmytina gathered in the palace hall waiting for Lady Christa discussing future advents. After a short wait Christa walked in through the doors and approached the table the others were sat at. Without saying a word she stepped beside the table and placed Shione's sword on the tabletop. Leon was the first to speak,

"That is Shione's sword mother, Where is he?" Christa walked over to her seat and calmly set herself down leaning back as if to relax,

"Shione has stripped himself from his duties. I have been told he has left the city. He won't be coming back." All was silent and again Leon was the one to question,

"Why has he left? Where has he gone?" Christa sighed loudly,

"He has left because of me. He believed my decision was wrong. I reacted harshly. I do not know where he has gone. This is the least of our worries at this time." Clemmytina began to sulk,

"Mister Shione was going to make me my own sword so I could battle like the others. It's so unfair." Christa smiled,

"I shall get you your own little sword Clemmytina." She frowned unimpressed,

"That isn't the same. I don't want one from you; I want one from Mister Shione." Christa ignores the comment,

"The rider will have got to the City of Shangedain this morning. Thus meaning Binor and Dante will be traveling back here by tonight. They will arrive here tomorrow night at fast pace with King Shudae and his people. We will not let them rest. We will move straight away toward the small port and follow as planned. Clemmytina, do you know how long it may take us to travel to the city of Seeyarta?" Clemmytina nods,

"We have a long way to travel really Miss Christa. We have to go down river until we reach the sea. We can travel from there almost in a straight line across the sea. If you could use your power Miss Christa and beg the winds help. A couple of week's maybe. I am sorry, I am not entirely sure." Christa looks up as if making calculations in her head,

"Everything will be fine. I can use my power to speed up the journey over the sea. Right, Leon, please can you continue to help with the city people and the soldiers getting ready. We need to rush to leave on time. Catherine, I want you to help me pack what is of use in the palace and my belongings." The three of them stand and Leon bows his head,

"As you wish mother, I shall start at once." Leon leaves the room to continue helping how he was asked. Lady Catherine and Christa were left at the table. Catherine picks up Shione's sword from the table,

"Mother, you're going to want to keep this." Christa looked at the sword,

"Why would I want to keep that Catherine? What use do I have with that sword?" Catherine places the sword back on the table as Clemmytina speaks up,

"What can I do? I want to help." With Clemmytina being the size she was Christa couldn't think of anything that she would be able to do. Catherine kneels down beside the table making herself at eye level with Clemmytina,

"Have you ever tried cooking any of your beans and mixing them?" Clemmytina shakes her head slowly,

"Would you like to try it?" Clemmytina takes a second to think,

"You mean mix up some beans to make a new sort of potion of some kind?" Catherine smiles,

"Do you know of any which you could make?" Clemmytina raised a mysterious cheeky smile,

"Do I? I know the mixture making the ultimate potion." Catherine continues to smile,

"And what does that do then?" Clemmytina jumps wildly to her feet,

"It makes me really big." She shouts while displaying a size spreading her arms out as far apart as she could. Catherine stands and Christa steps by her side,

"We will send someone to help you and get what you need. We look forward to seeing what you brew up." Clemmytina sits down,

"Ok, thank you." Christa and Catherine both leave the room and send the guard from outside the room to help Clemmytina with her cooking while they went and began to pack items worth taking on the long journey to follow.

Sure enough as Christa had thought, the rider arrived at the gates of the City of Shangedain. The rider dismounted from his horse and slowly walked between the dragons of Dante and Binor sitting either side of the gates. They both watch the man as he walked toward the gate. He didn't dare look at any of them because he didn't want to tempt any of them to try and eat him or attack him. So he crept to the gates and knocked as loud as he could. From inside he could here many men shouting at once. It was not shouting words he could here but more like grunts. The small shutter on the one side of the gate opened and a pair of eyes looked at the rider all over,

"I am a rider from the City of Savon. I have urgent important news for Dante, Binor and King Shudae from Lady Christa." The shutter closed and the gate was opened allowing the rider to walk in. The gate was closed again and the rider looked all around him to see large groups of soldiers standing in formation. Binor walks over to the rider,

"What brings you here friend?" The rider removes a small scroll from inside of his jacket. A Binor opened the scroll the rider continued to look around where he stood. He watched as Dante instructed a large group of well dressed soldiers on how to fight with throwing knives and a sword. Across the other side of where he stood he saw King Shudae checking off newcomers and issuing them with cloths armor and weaponry of there choice. Binor read the message on the scroll out loud as he read it,

"Dear Shudae, Binor and Dante, I have sent you this message to inform you that we shall be leaving this land very shortly. My instructions are that Shudae prepare his people for a long journey. Carry only what is needed. Leave as soon as you can upon receipt of this letter. Come straight to Savon and we shall all leave at once. Nobody has to stay behind. My high regards, Christa." Binor quickly walks over to Dante stamping his large feet as he did,

"Dante, we have to leave quickly. All of us." Dante turns and looks puzzled at Binor. He passes Dante the message and so Dante read through it. Dante walks with Binor over to Shudae. Tapping Shudae on the shoulder Dante pushes the message in front of his face. Shudae took a short moment to read carefully through the message.

"How soon is soon Dante?" Shudae asked with no emotion upon his face,

"We have to leave by nightfall. We know Christa well and this is what she would expect." Binor steps in front of Dante and places his hand firmly on Shudae's shoulder,

"My friend, It's time to say farewell to your city. We will help the best we can to get you and your people ready." Dante nods agreeing fully with Binor,

Trilogy of Leon

"Its going to be hard Shudae but what you must remember is your still the King and these are still your people. Lady Christa would not have sent this message if what she has planned isn't important." Shudae takes it within himself to do what is best and to follow the plan and advice of his new found friends and allies. Taking in a deep long breath he clapped his hands together,

"Well it is only morning so we have a good few hours to get ourselves sorted." The three of them disperse to groups of men and tell them to pass the word throughout the city to get everybody together. Put on red alert the city becomes fully alive with people becoming active. The whole city was woken as people packed there cherished belongings, food and water. The soldiers of the city all met at the front gates to get equipped as the women packed and the children watched in excitement.

Back at the Darkness City of Septhune Emperor Glenthoron sat with Lord Thain pack in Glenthoron's palace. They were waiting for the portals to become active so they could activate the attack upon the City of Savon. The army was almost ready and fully equipped but not all the beasts had been accounted for. Thain stood tapping his sword constantly on the dirty floor as Glenthoron sat on his throne thinking and waiting. The small goblin like creature which had given him the news about the failed attack on Savon entered the room and appeared in front of Glenthoron. He went down on his knees and clutched his hands together. Shaking the goblin spoke,

"Master, may I speak?" Glenthoron looks at him with his evil eyes,

Estaban Bridges

"No I rather you didn't but I'm interested in what you have to say so I guess you have to speak." The goblin stands and takes a few large steps backward,

"Well master, I have been informed of some disturbing news." Interrupted Glenthoron coughs and sighs,

"You always bring me disturbing news. Why you? How come there is never any good news? What is it?" The goblin looks down and seemed to embrace into a ball as he began to explain,

"The City of Shangedain Master, it's." The goblin pauses,

"It's what?" Glenthoron replies angered,

"It's changed over master." Glenthoron steps down from the throne and walks toward the goblin as the goblin retreats backward,

"In what way do you mean changed?" The goblin explains further,

"The people of the city have turned back to the light master. They no longer serve under your superiority master." Glenthoron shoots his staff forward toward the goblin as his eyes glaze over solid black. From behind his helmet he growls and with this the small goblin begins to shake violently. The goblin howls in pain as he is pulled from off his feet. Suspended in mid air one final howl was released as the goblins body exploded from within. Its body parts and blood spread around the floor of the throne room and up the walls and the ceiling with the force his body was ripped apart. Glenthoron stood without feeling for taking the small goblins life and looked over at Thain,

Trilogy of Leon

"How dare they turn there backs on me. They know they will be brutally punished for there treachery." He points at Thain,

"You will go and destroy these fools. Take whatever and whoever you need Thain. Make them burn, every last one of them? Understood?" Thain looks at Glenthoron,

"I shouldn't need that much of the resources. Your need more going after Christa and the others. I can handle such a small task." Thain leaves the room as Glenthoron sits back at his Throne. Thain proceeds through the palace and makes his way to the city gates. Standing looking over the large force he considers to himself what he could use to his advantage. He ordered a Goblin commander to prepare his group of ten thousand soldiers and beasts. As they stand strong to attention the oversized city gates are slowly opened and Thain walks with his army out of the city. Marching at a fast pace they move away from the city and the city gates were closed. Due to the soldiers and the beasts extended inhuman powers they began to sprint over the land. At the speed they traveled they covered long distance in a short amount of time.

The day passed on quickly. The sun began to surrender itself and move down through the sky as night moved quickly to take its place.

In the City of Savon preparation had been completed and the city stood at a stand still for the Shangerian people to arrive. Lady Christa sat in the throne room with Catherine, Leon and Clemmytina. They sat anxiously and in silence.

At the City of Shangedain preparation had also been completed and the city folk were all at the front gate waiting to leave. It had took sooner than expected to get prepared because the people didn't have that many belongings due to the fact that the darkness forces had took most of what they had. They had all worked hard and fast. It seemed that all of the people were more than happy to leave the city behind and start a new life. Dante and Binor stood ready to leave with the rest of the people at the front gate waiting for Shudae to appear. Eventually after a short time he appeared and stood between Dante and Binor. They looked over the soldiers now fully equipped and in full uniform and looked over the city folk. Shudae spoke freely,

"Quite a bunch of rare people wouldn't you say?" Dante laughed,

"You could say that friend but what a good bunch of rare people they are." The three of them turned and the gates were opened. The first to walk out was Shudae. Dante and Binor followed close behind and separated to each of there dragons. Shudae continued to walk and the soldiers began to emerge from within the city walls. The formation was that the soldiers would march in a constant block the best they could surrounding the city folk. Dante and Binor gave flight to watch over the migration from a bird's eye view, this being so that they could see any threat and to make sure all was going to plan. As they all marched at a steady speed the city became smaller and smaller in the distance. After a short while it could no longer be seen from where they had traveled to and the journey was making good progress. The night continued to come over the land as the people got closer to the City of Savon.

Early in the morning around three when the night was still dark Thain and his force came across the city of Shangedain. They had moved at such a fast sprint that they had covered an unimaginable amount of land. Believing the city was still occupied they stopped outside and got into a battle stance. Thain walked forward as the force stood ready for anything. The goblin commander stepped by Thain's side,

"It is ever so quiet my Lord. Have you seen the gates?" Thain runs his eyes over the top of the city wall,

"Yes I have seen the gate and I have noticed the same as you. I have noticed that the gates are slightly ajar. This bothers me." The commander looks up at Thain,

"Do you think that it is a trap Lord Thain? Do you think they expected us?" Thain grabbed the commander by his neck and pushed him toward the city,

"We shall find out once you enter, wont we?" Thain looks at the commander as he stares back at him scared. Knowing he had no choice he withdrew his sword and walked nervously toward the gates. When he got there he pushed the gate slightly and peered through. He continued and entered disappearing out of Thain's sight. A few moments passed and the commander reappeared with a large grin on his face amazed to be still alive. He shouted to Thain,

"There's nobody here Lord Thain. Nobody, the place is empty. It seems to be abandoned." Thain meets the commander at the gates and enters into the city himself. Having a glance around he turns to the commander,

"Open the gates fully and bring in the men and the beasts. We shall rest here. Let's just make ourselves at home shall we." The goblin rubs his hands together in delight once he had placed his sword back in the holster,

Estaban Bridges

"Indeed Lord Thain, at once." As agreed the commander pulled the gates open slightly further and walked out to the force waiting patiently. He raised his arms and said while grinning,

"Rest you filthy animals. The city is empty. Do what you want. Go where you want. Make yourselves at home by order of Lord Thain. The ten thousand or so men and beasts entered the city and the gates were closed behind them. The force ransacked the whole city trying to find anything of any value. The way they all saw it was, one mans rubbish is another mans gold and so not one stone went unturned as they worked there way through the city. Thain walked into Shudae's surrendered palace and sat down on the throne in the middle of a large dark room. He thought cunningly to himself about how he could begin his take over of the empire of Glenthoron's. He sat undisturbed for some time thinking over the endless possibilities he would face by being emperor and so he sat grinning to himself excited and faraway in his own ugly dream.

Time passed on quickly as Dante and the others continued on there journey. The people of the City of Savon slept. Those who could not sleep just lay thinking about leaving there homes. Thain and his force made themselves comfortable in the city Thain was taking as his own. Glenthoron made final preparations for himself as he tried to complete the portal spell but not having much luck with the size of the portals in which he was trying so desperately to open. Everything else was ready for him to make his drastic move and attack the city as he had planned so carefully. He was not ready to lose this battle. Not ready for the humiliation.

Trilogy of Leon

The night passed and the sun rose. Lady Christa and the people in Savon set final preparations for the suspected arrival of the Shangerians, Dante, Binor and Shudae. This was to be the last day for them in the city and so inside of themselves they said goodbye. The whole of the city stood without as much as a whisper. The people finalized what they had to but none of the people spoke. Maybe this was because they felt depressed and somewhat ashamed of leaving the city behind but what ever the feeling everyone felt the same.

Night soon came across the land once again. The silence of the city was broken when a shout of relief breaking the anticipation came from the front gates. The gates were opened and Lady Christa and the others were summoned. The large group of travelers crossed the moat bridge and halted outside the city. King Shudae, Dante and Binor made there way into the city leaving the two dragons perched over the city. They met with Christa, Catherine, Clemmytina and Leon at the foot of the palace steps. Lady Christa was the first to speak,

"Did you get here safely my friends?" All looking at each other Shudae replied,

"Yes Christa we did indeed. We set of as soon as we could after receiving your message. May I ask what the urgency is for?" Christa smiled,

"We are going to travel to the City of Seeyarta." There was a pause as Dante and Binor looked shocked at each other and Shudae frowned unconvinced. Clemmytina on Catherine's hand shouted out,

"That's right and I'm going to be the one navigating." Even more unconvinced they continued to stand baffled. Christa continued,

"We will be leaving this very minute. We are all prepared and ready to set off to the small port just down the river." Dante stepped forward looking past the others,

"And where is Shione may I ask?" Catherine answers for Christa,

"He has traveled in an opposite direction. We shall meet him again." Binor stepped level with Dante,

"Then why does your belt hold his sword on your side?" Lady Christa looked down and sure enough it was clipped onto Catherine's belt,

"He gave it to us so we could cherish it if he does not return." A royal guard soldier came across to Leon with Savior and handed him to Leon. Other horses were brought across and handed over to the others. They all climbed onto the horses and looked at each other. Christa smiles holding her powerful staff,

"We must leave at once. We here shall be those to one day thank for the lives we will save today as much as I would like to add Shione's name here, he abandoned hope. He cannot be honored. We shall return one day in the near future to reclaim this land." Lady Christa Began the movement as followed by the others.

The two city peoples joined in force as did two different armies. Two different cultures hand in hand moved for the good of the light. Clemmytina held onto Catherine's horse as they were riding across the drawbridge. She looked up,

"Miss Catherine. Don't be sad. We will all be better when we reach Seeyarta. There are no troubles there, just peace and beauty. I made some good mixtures while cooking; I used many beans and have made some magnificent potions." Catherine smiled falsely,

"I am not sad Clemmytina. I am just in deep thought. Maybe you can tell me about these potions on the long voyage ahead of us." Clemmytina looked back down watching the tracks in which they were making away from Savon. From up in the sky Dante and Binor watched over all of the people. The many people stayed close together and trotted along at a fast pace. The night was not very warm and the people would shiver. The image Binor saw as he flew in front of the massive moving crowd and looked back was magnificent to his eyes. The City of Savon stood now empty and lifeless as the people left it as a memory. At the front of the horde of people Lady Christa rode on her horse. Slightly by her side rode King Shudae and to either side of them were Leon and Catherine. They led the people on the journey with great power and leadership.

As the city folk, soldiers and the headship team went on there way they met the river and followed it toward where the port was situated.

Thain continued for his second night sitting at his new found throne. As his men and beasts were out around the city he sat alone still in his own little dream world of supremacy. A twinkle of light appeared in the corner of the room and Thain jumped to his feet clutching his sword and standing prepared and defensive. A small but bright light blinded Thain and so he shielded his eyes. When he looked back in the corner of the room a woman in a black tight uniform knelt,

"Sarahleene?" Thain questioned. The woman stood and walked calmly toward Thain,

"Hello Thain. How are you this late evening?" She asked running her hand through her hair,

"I'm actually quite fine thank you Sarahleene. Now, what are you doing here?" Thain raised his sword and placed it on the bottom of Sarahleene's chin as she approached further. She stopped and looked up into Thain's eyes,

"Cant I come and see my good friend when he is away?" Thain pushes up on his sword making Sarahleene's head move higher so she looked straight at him,

"The truth please, unless you do not value your life." She gives a small giggle,

"But Thain, you cannot kill me. You haven't got what it takes." Thain raised a smile on one side of his face,

"Is that so?" With this he used his power to pick her from the ground and hold her in the air so that her toes could just slightly touch the floor. She screamed and wiggled like a worm but could not release herself from his grasp. Thain growled and snarled,

"While I was dead in the depths of hell I learnt many things Sarahleene. Things Glenthoron never thought I knew or that I had the power to do. His mistake to himself was he brought me back to the surface of the land and he will fall to my power. He will be my slave. He will bleed his blood for me." Thain dropped Sarahleene and she hissed as she pushed herself from the ground. Slowly and cautiously she placed herself beside Thain kissing him softly on his neck. She ran her fingers smoothly and softly up and down his arms while running her tongue around his ear and breathing slowly. Thain remained in control although wanting to give into such seduction. With her one hand she reached down behind her small silk cape.

Trilogy of Leon

Keeping Thain's concentration on what she was doing, she slowly removed a small dagger from a holster on the back of her belt. Carefully she turned Thain's head gently and began to kiss him passionately and as she did so she brought the dagger around behind Thain while wrapping her arms around him. She lifts one leg as if she was taken away by the experience of kissing Thain and then strikes her wishful vital blow within his back. Thain shuddered and clutched Sarahleene tightly. He began to squeeze and apply pressure to her arms and so she stabbed him violently another two times. He slowly dropped down to his knees and released the hold he had of Sarahleene. As he leaned against her legs she took a step back and he fell to his hands and knees. Looking down at the floor blood drips from his mouth and he spat and choked. Sarahleene dropped the dagger in front of him. As it made a clang Thain looked up at her. His eye had become fully bloodshot as had his fake eye and his face was blemished red. His blood still dripped from his mouth and onto the floor. Sarahleene knelt before him and place her finger on his chin holding his head up for him,

"You're not that much of a big man Thain. Even a little woman like me has taken you down and now you're going to die. I am the one to stand by Glenthoron's side, not you." Thain smiles evilly and opens his mouth. The red blood dripping from inside strangely began to be replaced with a similar but black substance. Laughing deeply Thain rose from his hands and knees but without pulling himself up. He rose upright and his feet left the ground. He ran his hand over his face and reached for his fake eye. He pushed into his eye socket and removed the fake eye without feeling any pain and he dropped the eye onto

Estaban Bridges

the ground. In its place a small snake slithered from the socket and down Thain's face. Sarahleene had taken large steps backward horrified to see such a transformation. The snake which had come from inside Thain's skull dropped to the floor and slithered slowly toward Sarahleene. Thain laughed but coughed suddenly,

"You shouldn't have done that Sarahleene. You have made me angry, very angry." The snake stopped and stayed motionless but then it lifted from the ground and hissed rattling its tail at great speed. As it did so it seemed to slowly grow in length and to make room Thain stood back. The rattle snake grew to an unbelievable and extraordinary size towering high over Sarahleene and Thain. Sarahleene had now crawled into the corner and was trying to vanish herself as she had the power to usually do so. Thain shouted over,

"There is no chance of you escaping Sarahleene. You powers are nothing in the presence of me. Do you wish to die or do you wish to live." She does not answer and so to prompt a decision Thain clutches his hand signaling for the snake to snap at her in the corner. Without making any contact with her the giant snake snaps and hissed while rattling its tail as it hit the ceiling. A small amount of dust fell and so Thain brushed his shoulder. With no answer from Sarahleene he clutched his hand once again and so the snake snapped and took hold of her arm. The snake pulled her up and flung her across the room to the other corner. She rolled over and saw that the snake was quickly approaching her so she scuffled away and then sat kneeling. Crying and sobbing she pleaded with Thain,

"Please I am sorry Thain. Please stop." Thain placed his hand on the tail of the snake and ran his hand up its body as he walked calmly over to where she knelt. She looked up at Thain and watched in amazement as his eye socket scarred over and healed itself. Therefore he was left with one eye and the other socket healed over with flesh. She continued to plea for her life,

"Please. I shall be your servant master. I will do anything in which you ask." Thain padded the snake and so it slithered away. It lay itself down in front of the throne and twirled into a circle. It rested placing its head under part of its twirled body. Thain put out his hand smiling and so Sarahleene took it wisely. He helped her to her feet,

"You live for me now and you will do what I ask or I shall make you walk into a burning fire without a choice." Sarahleene put her hands on Thain's shoulders and he pushed her away,

"You do not touch me or come near me at any time Sarahleene. Sit below the throne and sit quietly. Your power will remain frozen until I need you to use it." He pointed to the throne. She remained silent walking over following the direction of his finger. She sat on the floor next to the throne looking at the snake next to her. Thain stood once again in deep thought about how he could use Sarahleene to his advantage but came to the conclusion she was not powerful enough and was easily excess material at his disposal.

Emperor Glenthoron stood in the middle of a circle of flames as he completed his spell and finalized the passageway. The portals to the outside of the City of Savon had now been opened. Because of a safety spell placed upon the moat of the city, the portals could only be opened on the outer side of the moat. Glenthoron rushed out of his palace and to the front gates of his city. Carrying his staff he approached one of two large black portals. He stood in the middle of the two portals and sent in the force of roughly two hundred and forty thousand soldiers and hell beasts. The courtyard had become completely empty and all had passed through the portals to the other side. Glenthoron took a long look over his city which he was leaving almost uninhabited. With more pressing matters at hand he also entered through one of the portals.

Stepping from the portal he had entered Emperor Glenthoron marched himself slowly through the incredible army arranging themselves into there places. Eventually all the beasts and all the soldiers were in position and Glenthoron looked at Savon unable to stop himself grinning at the though of victory. Noticing the drawbridge was currently down Glenthoron placed his hand on one of the goblin commanders heads,

"Oh dear for them, they haven't been expecting us." The goblin shook of Glenthoron's hand and stood forward. The goblin squealed loudly at the first large group of hell beasts. The beasts lined up next the drawbridge and made there way across. Glenthoron watched carefully to see it was a trap premeditated and was happy to see nothing come of the group crossing the moat. Before sending any more troops across Glenthoron thought wisely and got the goblin commander to also cross the moat to approach the city gates. Reluctantly the commander proceeds to carry out his orders and takes the group of hell beasts further toward the city gates. By getting so close to the city, Lady Christa was automatically issued with a warning through her sense. Before she had left the palace in the city she

Trilogy of Leon

had put a spell upon the city that if anything or anybody approached she would be warned.

Lady Christa stopped in her tracks as the journey to the port came to a stand still. Leon rod up beside her,

"What's wrong mother, why have you stopped?" Christa looked intrigued at Leon,

"Give me a moment please Leon." Leon became silent as Christa closed her eyes. She was able to join with the spirit of a small robin. The robin in question was the one she had sent to fetch Dante and Binor. The robin's spirit was happy to lend its help to Christa and so the Robin flew over the city. Christa could see out of the robin's eyes as if she was flying in its place. The robin flew to the front of the city and perched itself on the city wall so that it looked from the few of the city gates. Lady Christa saw the large army and the approaching smaller scout group. Relieving her from the trance with the spirit Christa looked over at Leon,

"It is a very good thing we left when we did Leon. There is such a large army outside of Savon's gates we wouldn't have been able to defend ourselves for long. We must move more quickly before they come after us. We have to get far enough away from them." The chase was on and the travelers sped up there movement. Christa thought to herself that they had to get to the port, before the darkness forces got to them. That way they would take all the ships leaving none for the darkness to give chase with. They all rushed and in advance Christa sent ahead Dante and Binor to clear the port from any possible opposition. As they quickly fled further away from the city Christa took the opportunity to set a magic spell to stall the darkness. As she rode she lifted her staff high into the air,

"The circle of water, the water of life, transform now to a circle of flame and the fire of death." The jewel on Christa's staff lit up and a small flame blew larger in the wind. With such a spell cast back at the City of Savon the moat began to bubble. Boiling it began to steam. Emperor Glenthoron stepped back wandering what was happening. The sound of boiling water could be heard and the commander, with the group of hell beasts stopped and turned looking back toward the drawbridge. Large balls of water flew up high above the ground and the whole army looked up watching there whereabouts. Glenthoron frowned confused. As the balls of water fell back down to earth they exploded into a pool of fire. The fire balls picked up pace and fell crashing into the ground and in the large groups of the army. The formation of the army began to break up as all of the soldiers and the hell beasts moved apart. A cluster of the fire balls came down at once and annihilated the group of darkness nearest the city gates. The fire balls flattened them into the ground and burnt them to nothingness. Glenthoron raised a spell to cover himself. A protective wall of solid earth covered him as he raised a separate spell. He made a spell so powerful that the ground began to shake. The wasteland over the drawbridge and around the city began to erupt and crack. Glenthoron then pulled the ground forward, covering the moat and extinguishing its boiling heat. All around the city the earth made a solid cover over the moat and the moat could no longer be seen. Glenthoron stood from under his earth shield and looked about his army. They had all scattered and now stood waiting, scared of anything else from happening, none of them moved. Glenthoron pointed his staff up in the air and brought it forward. He shouted loudly,

"Forward." All of the army of beasts and soldiers began to run toward the city growling and chanting at the tops of there voices. Glenthoron assisted with the charge and walked quickly. Across the rough ground he walked as his army ran past him. Stopping at the front gates Glenthoron looked across the city walls surprised not to see any archers or any defense of any sort. He knelt down in front of the gates a safe distance away. He propped his staff into the ground for support with it pointing directly to the gates. The way forward was clear as he started to whisper a spell,

"Lend me fire, lend me flame and break these gates before me." The top of his staff lit up brightly and a shot of explosive flame flew toward the gates. Upon impact the gates were blown into tiny splinters leaving an open doorway into the city. The army readied themselves once again but no soldiers, no magic, not a piece of dust or anything came from within the city. The dust settled and Glenthoron stood looking into the city. He walked forward confused and shocked. He got to where the gates once stood, peering his head through. He looked from left to right and saw nothing. Watchfully he continued further into the city and relaxed when he realized there was not a soul in the city. His ease soon changed to anger which changed quickly to extreme rage. Continuing throughout the city he looked to see if the people of the city were in hiding but still he found nobody. The army had remained at the front gates without entering and waited patiently for Glenthoron to come back or for a signal for them to enter.

Estaban Bridges

Eventually Glenthoron came to the foot of the palace steps. He twirled around and around raising his arms,

"Where are you cowards?" he shouted across the city,

"Come and fight me, come and defend yourselves against my army." He stood still with his arms still raised and looked down. Black clouds began to cover the land and floated above the city. The army at the gates remained where they were looking up into the skies. Glenthoron blinked and his eyes became pure black. As the clouds continued to blank out the moon and the stars Glenthoron roared. Wind began to blow furiously over the land and the ground began to rumble. Glenthoron held his staff with both of his hands and slammed it top down onto the ground. As it hit the ground, the ground around Glenthoron began to ripple. Expanding outward the ripples became larger and deeper in the ground. Buildings in the city collapsed with the ripples as the ripples went through them. Following the awesome destructive power of the waves over the ground Glenthoron pulled his staff from the ground and threw it away from him. He was left standing with his eyes blacked out. He looked around the city from where he stood as the wind continued to blow. The sky had now become fully covered with the black clouds and hardly any light was being let through. In a final act of rage, Glenthoron clutched his fist and smashed it against the ground with a harsh punch. From that point he had punched the ground a destruction of the city took place. From where he stood a ball of power and mighty magic grew. Everything it touched as it grew disappeared. It evaporated into nothing. The ball which grew out from Glenthoron standing in the middle grew

Trilogy of Leon

and expanded the size of the whole city. It grew further out disintegrating the city walls and it stopped when it reached the remains of the moat. His whole army had been wiped out in a smooth motion. The wind ceased to blow and all became silent. Glenthoron looked up from his kneeling position. Nothing was left. The City of Savon had been reduced to nothing more than a memory. Neither a brick nor a stone was left. What was left was unearthed ground, mud and dirt unevenly all around him. The power and the rage had left nothing. Literally all that remained in the perimeter of the city and inside of the ruble moat was Emperor Glenthoron kneeling in the middle of the area. He stood slowly and grinned to himself happy about causing so much demolition and killing his army made him laugh. Unfinished he looked up into the sky,

"I call you now oh master. Lend me your truly invincible servants. Let me have the help of your children. Your spawn, give them to me." Once again the ground shook violently. A magic portal opened and through it came a tall fully cloaked stranger. Its height was twice that of Emperor Glenthoron's. Nothing could be seen of his face and any part of his body. His hood covered the majority of his face and any gap was to dark to be seen through. The strange creature approached Glenthoron slowly taking small steps. It stood close towering over Glenthoron as he looked up remaining silent. The creature made a deep short growl and lifted Glenthoron from the floor by his neck. The creature spoke deeply,

"You call me to this land and you demand off me." The creature squeezed harder on the grip around Glenthoron's neck. He began to choke and so he tried desperately to speak out but was not able to. The creature lifts him up to full length into the air and then throws him down crashing him into the ground while still holding onto him. The creature applied pressure onto Glenthoron's body pushing him into the muddy soft ground,

"You do not demand off me Glenthoron." Releasing the pressure the creature peels him from the floor and holds him upside down by his legs and then lets him go sending him again falling to the floor. Quickly Glenthoron pushes himself to his feet and takes a few hard steps backward. Staggering he kneels down a short distance away from the creature,

"I am sorry my magnificent great one. Please I beg your forgiveness." The creature holds up his gloved hand to silence Glenthoron and it spoke,

"What have you done upon this land?" Glenthoron replied,

"I have many battles master. I need more help." The creature continues,

"Thain, Thain has betrayed you. Sarahleene has also betrayed you. You are foolish Glenthoron." Shocked Glenthoron questions,

"How do you know this? That is not true." The creature stepped forward and raised his voice angrily,

"I see everything and I know everything. You forget your purpose. You brought back to life a human, who is trying to take your power and your assassin, will now try to assassinate you" Glenthoron shakes frightened,

"Please master; give me the chance to redeem myself." The tall creature turns his back on Glenthoron and walks slowly back to the portal he had emerged from. Looking back the creature points at Glenthoron,

Trilogy of Leon

"Summon my sons Glenthoron. I grant you there service. If any of them suffer I shall make you suffer." Glenthoron stands as the creature continued,

"If I didn't have greater issues at hand over the ocean I would sort your idiotic problems out myself. I would have ripped you from your skin and drain you of your blood for the shame you have thrown upon yourself." The creature walks closer to the portal and Glenthoron shouts after him,

"Master, I will hunt the vermin out for myself with your sons help. I will follow them to where they have fled and we will destroy them." The creature turns quickly around and suddenly its eyes can be seen through the darkness of his hood. They glow red,

"You shall sort out the break in the links between your own chains Glenthoron. How do you expect to be victorious in battle against your enemies if your own ranks are shredded apart? The problems start at home Glenthoron. Once these are sorted you can undertake battle out of your land." Its eyes became dimmer,

"The battles I face over the ocean are more important than this disgrace of a small island. Once I have dealt with the land over the ocean I shall be back here. If you have not completed what I have asked then you shall die." The creature stepped back into the portal and the portal closed with a bright flash. Glenthoron was stood alone in the vast dark empty land. Excepting his masters offer he began to summon the children. He opened his arms to the skies and beckoned a spell,

"Appear before me sacred stones of power, stones of wisdom and the power of the ancients. Appear before me so I can summon through the doorway to hell." With the whole of the land covered in darkness the life force of the planet gathered and met at Glenthoron's feet. An enormous amount of light flashed and all became dark once again. The sky opened and rain began to drip. The breaking sound of thunder shot across the land as sharp lightning cut through the air spiking downward into the ground. The wind picked up to a great gale and the rain increased as the lightning became larger. With a giant roar of thunder the ground shook and Glenthoron fell to his knees. All around him large stones erected from within the ground. Firstly to appear was an almost perfect, unbroken circle of large stones. As these became fully erected and stable five individual sets of stones grew from the ground. Each of them consisted of two stones, standing and a large stone, sitting on the upright stones, making a solid outline of half rectangles, like in the shape of a doorframe. These grew in a similar smaller circle but with one in front of Glenthoron and two either side. These became fully stable and so a small stone alter emerged in the middle of the whole two circles. The shaking of the ground stopped and the lightning ceased to attack from the sky but the rain remained falling and the wind continued blowing hard and fast. Glenthoron stood to his feet looking around as what would become commonly known in the future as, Stonehenge. It was the doorway to hell, the passageway from hell to earth. With the means before him to summon the beasts straight from hell, Glenthoron stepped behind the stone alter and held onto each side tightly. Looking up into the sky he smiles evilly and removed a small blade from by his side. He cut across his other arm and his blood began to gush from the wound. It flooded over the stone alter and bathed

Trilogy of Leon

it staining the surface red. After dropping the blade he placed his hand over the wound and healed himself before he lost too much blood. Shouting once again he began his next spell,

"Here is my blood. Take my blood. There is much more blood across the land for you to feast upon. My blood is an offering and my blood is a sacrifice. I beg you please lend yourselves to me as your father wished. Lend me your power." Portals opened on top of each of the five doorway shaped stone structures and a creature appeared on top of the structure in front of the blooded alter. The creature was built large and its body red and flesh burnt. Its flesh clung to its body crispy and dry. Claws hung from the beasts fingers which were dripping with blood. The creatures head had numerous horns bulging from its head which were sharp like tusks and on the end of each of them blood dripped. Blood dripped from the mouth of the beast it knelt holding to the side of the structure with its one hand,

"You summon me with the grant of my father. I am Yuhun-des and I serve you." Glenthoron stood back and looked at the other four portals. Emerged from the others came other beasts. From one came a creature with large wings. From its spine came spikes all up its back. The creature had four long arms with instead of fingers three large bone claws on each hand. It hissed as its tongue like a snake rattled out of its mouth. It's hissed through its teeth,

"You summon me with the grant of my father, I am Sij-ectos and I serve you." From another of the portals emerged the third of the hell demons. This monster had two heads from its neck and was built larger than the

Estaban Bridges

others. Its muscles stuck out much further and it was covered in iron chains. The demon growled and both heads spoke,

"You summon us with the grant of my father, we are Feeg-kus and Feeg-ras and we serve you." Still not finished the forth of the brothers appears out of a portal. This creature was bull looking with a large tail wrapped around it; the beast balanced the end of its tail on the ground. On the end was a large iron ball of large spikes covered in blood, it spoke,

"You summon me with the grant of my father, I am Dak-elu and I serve you. Finally the fifth of the brothers appeared from the last portal. It seemed fairly normal with a human shaped figure but it had still very much muscle and its jaw was of a different shape. It came out a long way and its teeth were like razors. The last one spoke and introduced himself,

"You summon me with the grant of my father, I am Kul-jas and I serve you." The atmosphere had an instant change and the sky became clear. All of the dark clouds vanished. The rain disappeared and the wind went to nothing more than a breeze. The five beasts standing upon the stones all jumped down. Glenthoron remained speechless in amazement. He looked at each of the five beasts and though happily to himself that with these creatures he could do anything he pleased and kill all who he wished. Glenthoron spoke out,

"Thank your father, the chosen. We must move quickly, to Shangedain my brothers." The winged creature Sij-ectos lifted into the air and grabbed hold gently of Glenthoron. Running away from what is known as stone henge they all picked up pace.

Trilogy of Leon

The battle at Shangedain was going to be a great magical and bloody battle. The battle being between Glenthoron, with the five sons of the devil himself, versus Thain, Sarahleene and the small amount of dark soldiers and minor hell beasts. This battle would determine who was to go after Lady Christa and the others. This battle would be the decider of what could be the fate of Christa and the people.

With the summoning and the destructive wipe out of Savon passed Lady Christa, Leon and all the people approached closer to the port. They had felt the shaking of the earth but tried to ignore the fact that it could be danger. Christa knew that something terrible was happening to her city but she remained silent. The only thought that all of the travelers wanted on there minds, was that they were traveling to a place of safety. Some time passed after this as they nearly reached there goal.

Lady Christa had earlier sent Dante and Binor ahead to clear any hostility. They had then done so with ease. As Christa came to the top of a small embankment she could see over to the port. Flying high above was Dante and Binor on there dragons. To be safe Dante left Binor at the port and flew over to the position of Christa and the others. He hovered low and shouted,

"All is clear Lady Christa. The port was extremely empty to be honest. The only men who were here, we scorched." Lady Christa smiled and waved to Dante to say that she had understood. She continued further toward the port and the rest of the travelers followed. Dante and Binor set foot on the ground as everybody gathered at the port itself. Lady Christa, Catherine, Leon, Clemmytina, Shudae, Dante and Binor stood in a circle looking at each other. With Clemmytina being so small she stood on Catherine's palm. Christa relayed the plan,

"We have got this far and we have so easily. I am happy for our safety." Catherine butted in,

"Mother we are not safe yet. We still have far ago across the ocean."

"Catherine. Be positive and do not light up the negative. We have Dante and Binor following us in the sky. We have Leon and all the soldiers. We'll be fine." Clemmytina coughs as real as she could and as loud as she could. Leon raised an eyebrow,

"What's wrong Clemmytina, would you like to tell us something?" Clemmytina looks slightly over at Dante and Binor standing in the circle,

"There could be one tiny problem Miss Christa, about those little dragon things." Christa looks at Dante and Binor as they both frown,

"What about them?" Christa asked,

"Well they wont be allowed into Seeyarta and there is nowhere for them to stay. I am sorry but they must be left behind if Mister Dante and mister Binor wish to come with us." Christa looked over at them both. As they both look at each other they instantly knew there feelings and the decision they were to make. They took a step back and Binor spoke,

"We can't leave them. They have done so much for us and been with us through hell and back again." Dante agreed,

"That is the truth Lady Christa. I and Binor are both sorry but we cannot accompany you and the others any further." Upset but understanding Christa hugs the both tightly which they did not expect at the slightest,

"Dante, Binor, I thank you both for your help. I am glad you answered my calls for help and I am glad we met once again. I will miss you both but I promise we will meet again." Leon stepped forward and shook both of there hands firmly,

"In the time that we have known each other friends I have come to the conclusion you are both great men. Always look to the light and you will be safe. I hope you have safe travels and as Christa said, we will meet again in the future." Catherine stepped forward next to Leon and hugged them both. She moved beside Christa and put her arm around her smiling. In her other hand Clemmytina was sat down sulking and tiny tears rolling from her eyes. She said loudly through the tears,

"Bye Mister Dante. Bye Mister Binor. I hope you stay okay. Look for beans for me please and I shall fetch them soon." Cheering up she smiles as Shudae slaps each of them on the shoulder,

"Great haste friends. Be well." With this Dante and Binor mounted onto the dragons and leaped into the air. Dante shouted down at them all,

"We've got nothing better to do you know. So instead of just sitting down and doing nothing, were going to get Shione, take care friends." A small blast of flame from each dragon signaled fare well and they flew between the clouds disappearing quickly into the distance. Christa instructed Catherine and Shudae to continue the march toward the port. They could see many large ships docked safely and all of the people began to run to the ships which they wanted to travel in. The generals of the soldiers took charge of the amount of ships the best they could. Leon stood in the same spot as before with Lady Christa silent watching the city folk and soldiers boarding the escape carriages. Leon looked closely at Christa. She stood with a sad expression upon her face and she seemed to look beyond what was happening as if she were in her own dream world. She looked at Leon and into his eyes. Smiling looking at what might have been her only strand of hope. Leon spoke softly,

"Mother, you seem sad and distressed. Why be like that when we are all safe?" Christa sighed sadly,

"Shione left because of me. Dante and Binor have gone. The city of Savon I feel has been destroyed. We flee, scared. I run because I fear. With my retreat I take the people and the ones I care most about with me. I feel no matter what I do, I will never and cannot do anything right." Leon held his mothers hand gently,

"Mother, they may have left but they shall be back and so shall we. Nothing is your fault. Fate, destiny is what controls what happens in our lives. Have faith mother." Christa shook her head thinking the worst was yet to come,

"Faith, what is faith Leon? Faith is nothing more than a betrayed truth. If we all had faith would we be in the situation we are in now. Would I be running away if I had any faith at all? I believe the fact is I have lost hope Leon and those who lose hope lose life. They lose the purity of there soul and there is two options, the darkness or death. I choose death Leon. I would never want to live without the aura of the light. What is a life without a meaning? It's nothing Leon." He let go of Christa's hand and took a small step back confused and shocked from what he was hearing. Christa began to ride off toward the port and looked back with a serious look on her face,

Trilogy of Leon

"Kill me Leon, kill me son, if I ever begin to fall." She continued to the port as Leon remained motionless. He thought clearly and made an evaluation, this being that over his dead body would his mother fall into the trap of darkness. His body was to be laid out and not one drop of his blood was to flow before his mother gave up hope. He was to stick by this promise to himself.

All went well as Christa ordered the departure from the port. Many ships began to enter through the river to the open sea as they slowly sailed away. Lady Christa and Catherine were on one ship. Leon was on another with Clemmytina and Shudae sailed with some of his men on another. These ships sailed in front of the others. Like a mass swarm of bees they set sail into the open sea. Clemmytina gave directions to Leon so his ship became the leader in front of all the others. Clemmytina spoke to Leon,

"Mister Leon, do you think all will be okay? Do you have hope?" Leon smiled at the little creature sitting on the side of the boat holding on for her life,

"I have hope Clemmytina. What use is it if you do not have hope? If you have no hope there is no end." Clemmytina remained silent thinking about Leon's comment as on another ship behind Leon's, Christa and Catherine held each other tight looking forward into the endless blue. Shudae stood proud on his boat with a few of his soldiers as a man approached him from behind. The man moved silently as if drifting at stood close behind Shudae. He smiled,

"You've became good at that Lord Matius, still room to improve." The man wore cloths like a ninja. He had all black cloths with an old thin sword on his back. Cloth covered his face almost completely apart from his eyes. The man know as Lord Matius spoke deeply and sternly,

"Thank you King Shudae. Tell me, when can I meet the others?" Shudae smirked,

"When you're ready Matius and when they need your help. Until then you shall keep away. They must not know that you are Thain's son as of yet." Matius lent against a banister,

"Why do you think that they will not welcome me? I am on your side after all and I do not fear my father. I am just waiting for the opportunity to do to him what he did to my mother. The man must die as he killed my mother. He must pay for his sins." Shudae nodded,

"I agree my close friend and you shall get your chance. Wait until we come back to this land. Then you can battle Leon as you wished and find your father. I am still troubled by your reason for wanting to fight Leon." Matius turned and began to drift silently away,

"For the title Shudae, I am the better fighter between our two peoples. I just want to prove that our people are the most triumphant therefore becoming the reigning peoples when we return to our land." Matius disappears among the depths of the ship leaving Shudae to think of his priorities.

As the journey to a far away place moved swiftly on five hell monsters stood in a line outside of the City of Shangedain. Thain peered over the city walls and saw Emperor Glenthoron step forward from behind them. The emperor shouted fiercely at the top of his voice,

"Thain, we wait for you. Show yourself and fight us as you wish so badly to do." Thain walked calmly down to the forecourt and stood safely behind the city gates. Sarahleene appeared,

"What will you do master?" Thain looked up and his eyes had turned fully black and once again glazed over. All of the soldiers and the beast of Thain's had gathered at the forecourt waiting to go into battle. Weapons at the ready, all was silent. The tension began to mount and breaths began to run hard. The atmosphere became cold and still all remained quiet. The shaking of armor clinked as the soldiers began to shiver freezing in the cold and also scared. They knew what Glenthoron was capable of doing. Part of this was proven when bolts of fire flew shooting across into the city like shooting stars across the night sky. After the blasts of the fire balls the calmness set in once again. A very short moment passed as the gates began to shake and vibrate under pressure of Glenthoron's. Thain armed himself and pointed his sword forward. With a bright flashing light the gates shattered into millions of tiny pieces and after the light the five sons of the devil barged in. Glenthoron appeared inside of the gates and the great battle entered its wildest of times. Thain and Glenthoron stood in front of each other wielding a shielding force against one another stopping themselves from being thrown across the ground. They held each other at bay. Glenthoron growled at Thain and he shouted as the fight turned drastic,

"Traitor." He shouted as they flew toward each other at incredible speed. With a crash they engaged each other and the battle continued as it would for the next many endless hours. Who won was not decided as of yet. The battle just continued.

Estaban Bridges

Shione crossed vast lands approaching the north to where he would help on a different battle front. Still he was to battle against the darkness. He knew he would once meet his close friends once again. Soon he hoped. Shione continued to have hope and love in his heart for the woman he cared so much about. The some nights he slept he never dreamt of nothing more or nothing less of Christa. He lived for Christa.

Dante and Binor the close companions flew through the sky over the high trees and low stars. They flew to find Shione and aid him on his journey. They also hoped that they would fight for the light and help defeat the darkness. There hope lay in the depths of there hearts and for the willingness to do what mattered the most, for the good of the people and for the good of themselves.

Lady Christa and Lady Catherine, Leon and Clemmytina, Shudae and Matius slid without friction across the calm deep blue sea. Christa set a spell to heighten the power of the wind amongst the ships to quicken the journey toward Seeyarta. What they were going to see was the most beautiful, calm and magnificent sight anybody could ever see. A place built for peace, calmness, love and hope, the perfect home for Christa and the rest of the people.

In a faraway land, in an amazingly large building, with large pointing towers and decretive sculptures a large creature sat in a throne. His arms lay across the armrests and the creature breathed deeply. Out loud the creature thought,

"He must not fail me. The empire must not fail. It shall not be long until I must go to that land and take care of the troubles myself." Opposite from where the creature

Trilogy of Leon

stood many large creatures were being ripped apart and there skin removed as they were still alive. A large beast with gold teeth walked and knelt before the creature,

"Your meal my great majesty, I shall get preparation underway for your journey to the other land. I feel no remorse for those who you shall perish and burn. Show them that you are the true devil of hell master as you have done here." The beast stood and left leaving the devil sitting on the throne ready to cast his fire on the land he was to win for his own, for ever to be under his control.

In ten human months the future of the light is to be decided. In ten months the battle for light and dark will have its final bloodshed. All shall gather at the birthplace of the devil. The friends will reunite but at what cost will freedom cost them? Whose lives will be sacrificed for what matters most?

How can hope be kept if its fate is left in the hands of only a few?

The destiny will become known when, **Heroes Fight Hell.**

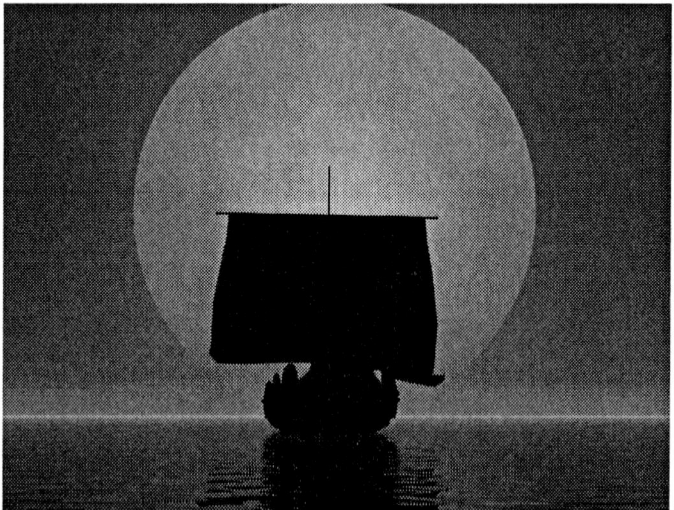

About the Author

Estaban was born in Shrewsbury, U.K. in 1987, the third son of a typically middle class family.

From a young age Estaban showed a great imagination through his writing of fantasy short stories and drawings; he also showed an exceptional skill for escapism through a multitude computer games.

Later in life Estaban grew into a personable young man, eager to learn new work based and life skills, starting full-time employment upon leaving school with

10 GCSE's reflecting excellent grades in all subjects; at the same time he continued to develop his writing ability to produce this 52,000 word, fantasy trilogy story, by eighteen years of age. We are sure you would agree this is an exceptional achievement for a young man, when considering today's pressures to conform to a stereotypical young person's behavior.

In time, Estaban will no doubt produce further works of fiction maybe even factual in the form of a Biography; he will most certainly publish the third story in the series namely: 'Heroes Fight Hell'.

We hope you enjoy this book and want to find out the conclusion to the trilogy by purchasing when released "Heroes Fight Hell".

"In ten human months the future of the light is to be decided. In ten months the battle for light and dark will have its final bloodshed. All shall gather at the birthplace of the devil. The friends will reunite but at what cost will freedom cost them? Whose lives will be sacrificed for what matters most?

How can hope be kept if its fate is left in the hands of only a few?

The destiny will become known when, **Heroes Fight Hell**".

Mr. Estaban C Bridges Esq.